ANSLEY CALLOWAY

Following Fox

First edition

This book was professionally typeset on Reedsy.
Find out more at reedsy.com

To the women who aren't sure if he's the one, break up with him. You'll know for sure when the relationship is over.

Contents

1

Charlotte

Yesterday I set flame to the vows that I spent far too long writing, sold my flashy diamond ring to a pawn shop, and returned my wedding dress. Alexander James Merriweather and I were supposed to be married in two weeks, on July 11th, in front of all of our friends and family. But our future went up in smoke, and I was reminded that love always comes at a cost.

The events before that were all a blur, but I do remember being sick from trying out a new food truck for dinner. My big fancy corporate job in the city didn't take kindly to us using sick days, and my rival coworker was also constantly looking for reasons to feed our manager as to why I shouldn't get another promotion. So I went to work anyway.

Around lunch I finally bowed out as I was contemplating how embarrassing it would be to throw up on the boring gray carpet. I gathered my belongings and returned an overly enthusiastic wave from my asshole coworker on the way out. His condescending smile stuck in my mind as I began the walk home with my heavy work bag thrown over my shoulder.

My keys jingled while I shoved them into the front door of my new shared apartment with the supposed love of my life. This was the first time I had ever shared a space with a significant other and the place still felt unfamiliar. My cheeks felt warm and my palms were sweaty as I slid the keys back into my work satchel. I took another deep breath and I pushed open the door making sure to shut it hard so the lock would stick.

Footsteps quickening, I speed-walked to the bedroom. I passed several boxes of varying fullness and stepped around a few piles of books to make it to the door. Alex lived here for years without me, so the space felt already complete without the addition of my belongings. My things were strewn around with no real place for them yet.

My flushed ears were ringing by the time I finally opened the door to the bedroom. Feeling weak and even more nauseous in this apartment that didn't feel like home, I stepped inside the doorway.

And then I looked up. Lips parting into a gasp, my eyes widened. The ringing in my ears turned into dead silence. The loud screech of the door as I pushed it alerted the two people fucking in my bed to turn and look at me. All I saw was Alex's face staring at me all sweaty and horrified, as if a spotlight was on him.

Motherfucker. I opened my mouth to say exactly that, when the bile I had been holding down came up all at once. My puke covered the floor in front of the bed, their feet, and the beautiful white comforter I picked out before I moved in. After that, my instincts kicked in.

All thoughts and feelings flooded out of my body. This

suddenly was a familiar situation that left me on my own once again and thankfully, I had plenty of practice with handling difficult situations by myself. So I let myself feel numb and the logical side of me took control.

Their frantic voices carried into the bathroom as I finished puking into the toilet. I didn't even bother to brush my teeth after wiping my mouth with a towel near the sink. In the mirror, my eyes were underlined with dark circles and my skin had whitened into a sweaty pale sheet. The front strands of my dark hair stuck to my forehead. Some people would say I looked like I saw a ghost, but I really looked like I could *be* a ghost and star in my very own horror movie.

My feet carried me out of the bathroom into the living room where all of my things surrounded me in boxes. Never the sentimental type, there wasn't a ton of stuff in them other than clothes and necessities like books and toiletries.

The ringing in my ears returned as Alex followed me through the apartment. I could tell he was talking to me through the muffled sounds, but I didn't bother trying to listen to him. Stumbling around the apartment, my arms were quickly filled with the most important things I could think of at the time including a backpack filled with clothes from the nearest open box, my work bag, and a pint of ice cream.

He called after me, but I couldn't even look back. I was certain I would blow chunks at the sight of his face again. My long legs swiftly carried me through the city without any sort of plan, and somehow I wound up on the doorstep of a familiar building.

I pulled out my phone to call the only person on the planet I would want to see right now. Phone pressed to my ear, I forced my voice to steady before talking, "Dyl, are you home?"

"Of course I am. Turns out being a receptionist is so damn boring, and the men kept asking me to do things like I was their personal assistant. So I quit. Aren't you working?" She asked.

I blew out a breath and focused on the nice breeze. It was a hot day, and I was in a dress shirt and pants, so the wind felt like sweet relief. "Can I come up? I'm outside."

Dylan squeaked, and I heard what I assumed was her moving things and racing down the stairs. Seconds later, the door in front of me opened and I was faced with my best friend. She gasped, "You look like complete shit."

I forcefully laughed and moved to walk through the doorway. As we walked her worried stare didn't move from my face. "What the hell happened? Are you sick?"

That was the least of my worries now. "I tried out that new food truck on Third. Pretty sure they tried to poison me."

She took the ice cream container from my arms and carried it in one hand, opening the door to her place with her other. Carefully choosing her words, she started slowly, "Okay, what's with all of the stuff then? Is Alex working, do you need me to take care of you?"

I let out another deep breath and set my backpack and bag down before slipping my shoes off. I walked through her hallway to the living room and sat on the sofa. My head tilted back to stare at the ceiling as I counted to ten. Ten seconds to breathe and then I needed to act. React.

The freezer door shut as Dylan put the ice cream away and I heard her mumble something about it being melted. She joined me on the couch and gave me space to think as she sat quietly. I stood up to grab my laptop from my work bag before sitting back down. Finishing pulling up my work email,

I looked over at her.

"Hey Char, what's going on?" Dylan's voice sounded uncharacteristically timid.

I took a deep breath. Robotically, I recapped the last hour that had changed my life. "I felt sick, so I went home early from work. Alex was fucking another woman in our bed, so I grabbed my things and left. Oh, and I puked on them."

Her laugh in response was short and filled with disbelief. My fingers began typing as she stood up to take in the information. Dylan paced for a minute before taking in a gulp of air to announce, "That motherfucker! I'll kill him. I'm going to go over there and make him suffer."

I laughed quietly. "It's fine, I'm glad I found out before we were married."

"He is such a nickel. A dull, gross, dirty, worthless nickel," she seethed.

The first time I met Alex was at the restaurant Dyl and I worked for together, years ago. After he ate alone at one of my tables for over an hour, asking for more refills than I could keep track of, he left me a nickel as a tip along with his phone number.

Ever since that day, Dylan had called him the not-so-loving nickname of Nickel. She even called him Nickelback for a year straight after he insisted on going to a few concerts with me and Dyl in the beginning of our relationship. Although, when we got engaged I managed to convince her to back off a little bit.

Reminiscing on the past, I realized there were probably a few glaring issues with the man that I glossed over because it was easier than facing them head on. But that was all in the past now.

Dyl stared at me while I finished up my email. I hit send and pushed the laptop onto the table. My gaze locked onto hers as I leaned back against the couch to debate my next steps before she spoke again.

"What do you need? Do you want to cry or run off to another country? I would say we should go out tonight and find someone better but you don't look well enough to go clubbing." Her head tilted to the side and I considered her offer. Running to another country honestly didn't sound all that bad.

I huffed, "I want ice cream, but I won't be able to hold it down."

She laughed and pushed the back of her hand to my forehead. Bouncing up off of the sofa again, she called, "You're burning up, let me get you some medicine."

I heard her rummaging around through cabinets. Unlike my shiny high rise apartment with Alex, Dylan's place was not always neat and tidy. She kept far too many things, including a collection of napkins from every restaurant she went to. Her habit of trying out a new hobby every week was evident in the cluttered bookshelves that held a mix of video games, art supplies, and objects I didn't even recognize. She was one of the most unorganized people I had ever met. We both thrived in chaos, but Dylan's chaos was much messier than mine.

She returned with two pills and a glass of water in hand. "Do you want your coaster to be from Freddy's Chicken Wings or Cantina Bar and Grill?" When I shrugged she walked over to her overflowing napkin holder and picked out whatever was on top. Setting the napkin on the table in front of me she ordered, "Take this, it'll help with the fever."

I obeyed and grabbed my laptop when my brain wandered

off to the apartment. Alex's name was on the lease, so I should be able to leave with no issue, but I needed to cancel the wifi and his phone from my bill. In minutes, his name and address were removed from any of my bills and I was free. Financially, at least.

I mentally thanked myself for being overly cautious with everything. He insisted on putting both of our names on that apartment when I moved in, but I stood my ground. It made me wonder if he was doing it on purpose to trap me in the situation in case I found out about his dirty little secret.

Dylan pulled me out of my analysis. She gently took my laptop and closed it before sliding it back in my work bag, and putting it by the door. "So, what exactly were you doing just now?"

"I quit my job and removed him from any of my bills," I deadpanned. The glass of water was already starting to get sweaty on the table, so I took another big gulp. I set it back on the table and started fiddling with a button on my shirt.

My friend sat back down and turned her body toward me. Her hands grabbed my clammy ones and she waited until I held eye contact. "I absolutely love that you're trying out the whole living freely thing. Trust me, I am tied down by no man and no job." Her hands squeezed mine and she hesitantly smiled. "But didn't you work really hard for that position? You seemed excited about it."

I softly pulled my hands away and rubbed my sweaty palms on my pants. I sighed, "I just wanted to prove that I could do it. And I did. I got the job. But there's no way I'm staying here in this city with him."

Accounting was never a passion of mine. Or anyone's I supposed. It was a stable job that would pay well after college and required minimal risk. That was why I picked it, and when Alex mentioned his parent's firm was hiring new graduates I jumped at the opportunity.

A couple of years later and I had climbed the ranks from being an intern to a full time salaried position. It was the first time in my life that I had a stable income and it felt sweet. Stability quickly became a goal in all aspects of my life, which was why I was happy to settle with Alex.

While it was nice to see my significant other at my job before, now the idea of it seemed more like a nightmare. Even the thought of accidentally running into him made my skin crawl. How amazing is it that in one second a person can go from being the person you love the most to the person you hate the most. I would never be able to look at him again without liquid rage flooding my heart.

Dylan's eyebrows were raised. "You're leaving the city? Where will you go?"

I shrugged. "My grandmother left the cafe to me. I was putting off dealing with it, but there's no way I would run into Alex in Rosewood. I doubt he could even find it on a map."

I set the now empty glass down after gulping down the rest of the water. My fever was already lessening, as if the relief of having a set plan cured my sickness. Going back home felt daunting before, but in comparison to the mess here, living in Rosewood for a bit looked like a piece of cake.

That perked Dyl back up. She chirped, "I want to come. You know I've been dying to see this cute little place that you come from."

My eyes rolled and I reached for the remote. "Rosewood is little, but it's not cute. You're picturing Stars Hollow from Gilmore Girls, and it is certainly not that."

Any potentially charming aspects of the town I came from were lost on me during the years I lived there. I had much more concerning issues on my mind like where my mother ran off to or how I was going to graduate high school. Admiring the cute little shops and making friends with quirky townspeople wasn't exactly high on my to do list.

Pushing thoughts of the past aside wasn't easy. Especially now that I felt everything was up in the air again. I could not go back to the constant state of survival that I was in growing up, but I had a plan in place. And there was not much I could do right now other than ride out the rest of this nasty food sickness.

Dylan and I spent the rest of the day watching baking competitions on TV. We even turned it into a drinking game with a bottle of red wine she borrowed from her last job working at a wine tasting company. She did her best to distract me from the chaos that quickly took over my life, and I would be forever grateful.

The next day was back to business, and she came along to return the wedding dress and pawn off my engagement ring with a big rock on it. That night we lit a candle and set the vows I kept stuffed in the bottom of my work bag on fire.

After the words that no longer had meaning were burned and forgotten, Dyl dropped me off at the parking garage outside of Alex's apartment where I last left my car. I opened the trunk and shoved my few remaining belongings inside of it. The car was a bright blue color that always stood out in a parking lot. It was the first thing I bought after finally landing a steady job, and the first time I splurged on something when I could have bought an older model.

Turning away from the car, I gave my best friend a hug.

Saying goodbye to Dylan wasn't easy, but I knew I would see her again soon. She was practically my only family.

I turned my phone back on to use GPS and hundreds of calls and messages popped up. Quickly blocking his number, I pulled up the navigation app again and typed in the address to my late grandmother's cafe. And before I knew it, I was on my way to Rosewood.

Hours later, I made it within city limits and got out of my car to walk toward a familiar building in the dead of night to unlock it. Keys loudly jangled as I fumbled with the lock. A door next to the one I was trying to open swung open and I flinched. Then a large figure stepped out of the darkness and held up a baseball bat to swing.

2

Nick

My store was being broken into. After almost a full year of owning my business, one of the things I dreaded was finally happening. Rosewood was a safe place, but getting robbed happened in even the safest of places. Banging sounds were audible through the window next to my bed which meant someone was in the back alleyway. I threw on pajama pants and sprinted down the stairs of my apartment.

The closest thing I had to a weapon was a baseball bat one of the guys left here months ago. I grabbed it before throwing open the back door to face whoever it was that was breaking in. It was dark and there was only one street light that illuminated the back alley behind my store.

I squinted to let my eyes adjust to the low light. In front of me I found not a masked man, but a frazzled woman huddled by the door to the shop next to mine. She had bags hung over her shoulder and back, and the whites of her eyes were directed right at my bat.

We stared at the bat together for a second before I lowered it. My brain was still foggy from sleep so I muttered, "Why are you breaking in?"

She let out an outraged huff of air and turned back to her door. She held a filled key ring and proceeded to jam them in the lock one by one, loudly clanging the keys together as she worked through them. When the third key wasn't a success she kicked the door for good measure. That must have been why I thought my store was being broken into, she was being damn loud.

I stared as her movements were more and more panicked. She turned to me again and shrieked, "Can you go put on a shirt at least? I don't need some shirtless freak staring at me in the middle of a dark alley at this time of night."

"I live here, and your temper tantrum woke me up. If you don't want concerned visitors, maybe try to keep kicking doors down to a minimum."

Stepping closer, I squinted to see if I recognized her and stopped in my tracks. Those green eyes and that familiar scowl made my heart skip a beat. Her gaze narrowed at my face too as I stepped into the light. "Holy shit, Reid?"

"Fox," I breathed out quietly. My body stilled and my anger washed away into disbelief.

"Jesus Christ, did you join an emo band or something? I didn't even recognize you with that hair. Must have taken a dark path for you to get into hair dye over the past few years," she snarked.

Her eyebrows raised with a relieved smile. I guess even the elusive Charlotte Fox got a little nervous in a dark alleyway with a stranger holding a baseball bat. Charlotte had always looked her most confident when she was teasing me back on the volleyball court, this must be her happy place.

I ran a hand through my dyed dark brown hair. The truth was that I dyed it a few years back after my niece kept mixing up my twin brother and I. He always had a pitiful puppy dog frown on his face when Ruth called me daddy, so I dyed it to make the difference between us obvious.

"That makes two of us. You're sneaking into town at one in the morning. Can't be a good reason for that, can there?" Her face darkened, and I immediately regretted my words. I meant to mimic her playful tone, but I always managed to say the wrong thing around her.

In high school it was easier to hide my never ending curiosity about her by challenging her on the volleyball court. While she was shy, she was also competitive as hell and always fell for my taunts. The rivalry we shared back in school awarded me the honor of being one of the few people Fox spoke to. But now the same tactics felt childish and out of place.

It had been nearly ten years since I'd seen her. She always captivated me back then, and I would be lying if I said I wasn't secretly hoping that buying the place next to her grandma's cafe gave me a shot at seeing her again.

Today was finally that day. And I had already managed to fuck up in under ten minutes. I sighed and scrubbed a hand through my hair. "Hold on. I've got a key, I'll go grab it for you."

She remained silent and held the back door to my diner open for me as I rummaged through my junk drawer. I found the key to the cafe and walked past her to unlock it.

"My grandmother gave you a key?" She sounded suspicious.

I looked at her over my shoulder. "Yeah, Evangeline gave me a lot of advice my first year of business. We helped each other out, so she gave me a key in case I ever needed it."

During that year I had also made a few attempts to ask how Fox was doing, and learn more about her. But her loving grandmother was tight lipped on the subject, so I assumed that meant she was just as in the dark as I was. The older woman was kind and shared stories with me about nearly everything else in her life other than her granddaughter.

Charlotte's eyes followed me as I opened the door and gestured for her to walk in. I flipped the lights on and was met with a backroom filled with empty shelves and boxes. She took a second to look around before setting her bags on a table.

"Thank you," she sighed.

I nodded. It was probably time for me to leave, but my curiosity kept me in place. "Are you staying in town? Where are you planning on sleeping?"

"I'm staying here, there's a couch upstairs." An unsure pause. "Or there used to be. I hope it's still there." She crossed her arms and nodded towards the stairs.

There really must be an awful reason for her coming in during the middle of the night like this. She looked exhausted, and much paler than I remembered. Her t-shirt was crumpled, and her dark brown hair was half in and half out of her ponytail as if she drove with the windows down the entire way here.

I was tempted to invite her over and give her a proper place to sleep in my bed, but the Charlotte Fox I knew would only accept that as an insult. Though this Charlotte looked much more defeated than the one I was used to.

"Well, if you need anything I'm right next door. Just knock. Or bang on the wall since we share it." I pointed at the wall to my left where the buildings were pushed up next to each other.

She looked shocked. Her arms uncrossed with another sigh. "Okay, thanks Reid. I appreciate you not decapitating me with your bat."

My eyes rolled and I headed out the door. "Lock it behind me, you never know what five foot nine criminals wearing Care Bear t-shirts are lurking around trying to kick your door down."

Her signature deadpan stare brought a smile to my face. Familiar sarcasm filled her voice, "Ha, funny as always. How ever will I sleep at night?"

I shut the door at that and waited to hear the lock click before heading inside my own. Charlotte Fox was finally back in town after nearly ten years of wondering where the hell she had gone. Seeing her in person brought back all of those same feelings of stomach aches and head spins that I had back in high school. I could never keep up with her snarky comebacks and wicked serves.

Heading up the stairs, I pulled out my phone. It was too late to call anyone, so I pulled up my messages and sent a quick text to Kelsey asking her to come over in the morning.

I looked at the clock again and watched it turn to two. My bed welcomed me back, and I hoped to God that when I woke up in the morning this wasn't all some kind of a shitty fever dream.

Around six AM, a pissed off looking Kelsey strutted into my diner with a familiar hoodie hung in the crook of her elbow. She walked up to the counter of my diner and stared, waiting for me to speak first. I took a deep breath and reminded myself to do this quickly and respectfully.

"Hey, Kels. Do you want some coffee? I need to talk to you about something," I said.

She shoved my hoodie on the counter and moved to sit down on a stool. "No thanks, I already had coffee. Go ahead."

Looking around the mostly empty diner, I walked around and sat in the stool next to her. My body faced her and I spoke softly, "I think we should date other people. You're great and I have really enjoyed getting to know you, and spending time with you, but I don't see this going to a place that's more serious. And I know you're looking to get married, so I don't want to waste your time."

I paused to make sure I covered all of my bases. She didn't look shocked at all, her face remained even as she held eye contact with me.

Kelsey and I had only been on a few dates, but she made it clear from the start she was looking for a serious relationship. At the ripe age of twenty nine I figured now was as good a time as any to settle down. After my brother Ashton fell in love, I did wonder what it would be like to be in a relationship, and Kelsey was a great girl.

But seeing Charlotte again struck a chord. No one had ever come close to her. Not in the ten years we were apart had anyone stayed in my thoughts anywhere near as much as Charlotte did. And it was a dick move to string Kelsey along if I knew I was interested in someone else.

My still sleep-ridden brain screamed at me to see the logic. All night I stayed awake, going over this decision, and how insane it was. Charlotte could be married for all I know. Was she wearing a ring? I didn't even think to look, but either way I knew for sure Kelsey was not the one for me. There was no spark.

"And you decided this at one in the morning?" She sounded pissed.

16

"I'm sorry. I just wanted to tell you as soon as I realized, that's why I texted you so late. Maybe I should have waited until the morning to ask you to come over." I ran a hand through my hair. "You knew?" My eyes trailed to my sweatshirt on the counter.

She laughed forcefully. "Yeah, you texted me in the middle of the night saying you 'needed to talk'. Did you cheat on me or something?"

Well that was out of left field. "Hell no, why would you think that?"

"You texted me at one AM in a rush to break up. I imagine you just fucked a woman and decided she's worth keeping around, or you're about to and don't want to 'technically' cheat."

"Nothing like that happened. I was in my diner alone, and I just had an epiphany and wanted to let you know." My head fell as I tried to think of how to fix this. I really needed to get better at this relationship thing if I ever wanted a shot with Fox. "We can talk about it more if you want. I know you want to get married and-"

"No thanks, Nick. I've heard more than enough. We aren't going to work out, so there's no point in going over the boring details as to why." I opened my mouth to respond, but she already stood up and was walking around the counter to the back of the diner.

Following her through the kitchen, I spoke again, "Where are you going?"

"I brought over a bottle of wine we never drank last week. I'm going to get it."

"Okay, that's fine. Why don't you let me grab-"

She cut me off with a hand on my chest and walked to the

stairs that led up to my loft. Leaving a woman I just broke up with alone in my apartment seemed like a bad idea, but going up there to be alone with her seemed like an even worse idea. Minutes later she walked back down, her alcohol in a tote bag, and left the diner without a second glance at me.

Well that was the shortest breakup of all time. I caught a few customers staring at me after witnessing the interaction, so I picked up my hoodie and walked to the back again to catch up on paperwork.

3

Charlotte

The muscles in my back were stiff and sore as I rose from my makeshift bed for the night. Bright light streamed in through the windows in the loft apartment. I walked over to shove the sheer curtains fully open until the room was bathed in the morning sun. My eyes squinted until they adjusted to the brightness and I looked around to take in my new living space.

This building held a strong sense of nostalgia. The red brick was beautiful and worn. Layers of paint coated the wall by the window from the previous Rosewood residents that this room housed over the last one hundred and fifty years.

My grandma died over eight months ago, but surprisingly the place wasn't dusty at all. The last time I stood in this building was over ten years ago. After my high school graduation, I thanked my grandmother and gave her a check with as much money as I could live without. She kindly refused, but I left her with the check anyway.

She took me in and gave me a place to stay out of the kindness of her heart. When the scrawny, freshly thirteen year old me showed up on her doorstep claiming to be the daughter of her estranged child, she took one look at me and invited me inside. I was only looking for a place to stay, but she did her best to make it feel like home.

My grandmother and I didn't meet until I was thirteen, but she made a huge impact on me the five years that she was in my life. Her calm and sure disposition gave me hope for my future. The kindness she showed everyone encouraged my own to grow. She was the best role model I ever had, and she lived and died believing in love more than anything.

The records filled with love songs left on her coffee table proved that. Evangeline Fox listened, read, and practiced love as if it was gospel. The last words she said to me were 'follow your heart' before I walked out the front door with nothing but my backpack and old beat up car.

My mother had taught me lessons about love too. Those were much harder lessons, though. Ever since I could remember, my mother loathed the idea of being a mom. She taught me that people will love you when they have something to gain and will leave the second it benefits them. That was how I ended up on my own at thirteen years old.

I had a job delivering newspapers when I turned twelve that gave me just enough money to keep me fed during the weeks she disappeared. Though, that only seemed to encourage her to leave for longer amounts of time. When she spent a couple of months away after my thirteenth birthday and failed to pay rent on time, I was the one left on the street.

My head pounding once again reminded me of my dehydrated state thanks to that awful food I ate. I slowly walked downstairs tracing the floral wallpaper lining the hallway with my hand. Every inch of this place was a memorial to Evangeline. The walls and floors still smelled of her overpowering perfume.

Once downstairs, I walked into the front of the coffee shop and fumbled around until I found an unopened bag of pre-ground coffee and an already plugged in machine. The counters were clean here too. Everything was clean and organized the way I remembered when I worked at the shop back in high school.

Coffee brewed while I continued exploring the place in the daylight. A closed sign hung in the front door as if my grandmother was going to walk around the corner any minute and flip it around to start the day.

Dark hardwood flooring gave contrast to the mostly white cafe, there were a few white tabletops scattered around the dining area with black metal chairs to accompany them. The only color to be seen in the cafe was the giant side accent wall that contained more wallpaper with a busy, pink floral design.

My exploring ended when the coffee pot finished and I rushed over to pour myself a mug. Typically, I liked a splash of cream in my coffee, but if there was any still in the store, it had expired long ago.

I used my arms as leverage to lift myself to sit on a countertop to face the huge front windows of the store. Blowing into my mug to cool off the drink, I watched the street in front of me. People and cars passed by, showing life had never stopped in Rosewood all this time. Ten years and nothing had changed except for me. And the fact that my grandmother was dead.

The town felt empty without her. I never had many friends here, but Evangeline was a constant. A predictable figure to give advice when I didn't ask for it and always push me to go out and be present in my community. She wasn't just big on romantic love, but all kinds of love. I knew she felt sorry for me, but I did just fine on my own back then.

As I took my first sip of coffee, my phone vibrated. I pulled it out of the jeans I slept in and answered Dylan's call. She started talking immediately, "You make it okay?"

"Yep, I'm here in small town wonderland. Would you believe not a single thing has changed?" Which reminded me. Nicholas Reid was at my back door last night. Maybe one other thing was slightly different.

"Well what the hell are you planning on doing? Hiding out and walking down the yellow brick road every day? I know you're loaded from your fancy accountant job, but surely you'll need money eventually." I rolled my eyes. Just because Dyl couldn't hold down a serving job didn't mean my stable corporate job was *that* fancy.

I sighed, "I have savings, so I'll be good for a few months." I looked around the coffee shop. Evangeline had left me two things when she died, this shop and a note reminding me that love conquers all. "If I need to, I could always open the shop and make money that way."

Dylan gasped. "Open a coffee shop? For real? Can I come work there? That sounds like my literal heaven. Living in a cute town and I get to spend all day with my best friend."

I snorted and couldn't help but laugh. "No offense, Dyl. But I would never hire you, last week you bragged about calling in sick to wait in a virtual line to buy Taylor Swift tickets."

"Those tickets were so worth it. They're a once in a lifetime opportunity!" She defended.

She trailed off into an explanation on how concerts were far more important experiences than working. But my mind wandered as I looked around the shop. I really could open it up and continue Evangeline's business. She taught me all of the ropes, so I knew how to do everything on my own.

"Char? Are you even listening?" She said exasperated. I nodded even though she couldn't see me.

"Yes, yes. Just thinking," I absentmindedly replied.

Dylan's knowing laugh pulled me out of my thoughts. "You're making a plan. It must be a damn good one. Let me know when you've pulled off some great feat and became mayor of Rosewood."

Her click came before I could even say goodbye. I sat quietly stewing over my options for the store. When Evangeline left it to me, I planned on just selling it. I was engaged at the time, and had no plans of ever working on it in Rosewood.

For eight months I put off making an appointment to start looking for buyers, but maybe there was more reason to my reluctance than not wanting to visit Rosewood. Selling the place felt wrong. The shop had been here for almost twenty years, and I didn't want to be the one to break that streak. And even though I was the least sentimental person, something in me enjoyed the idea of carrying on a family tradition.

After finishing my coffee and washing out the mug, I went to the bathroom to fix my hair the best I could. My reflection in the mirror was a hot mess. Flyaways stuck out everywhere even as my hands did their best to smooth out my hair. The t-shirt I had worn for almost twenty four hours had a few stains from when I ate in my car, and was wrinkled from sleeping in it.

I sighed and gave a last pull at my ponytail to tighten it. My appearance would be dealt with later. For now, my curiosity got the best of me as I unlocked the front door of the Rosewood

Cafe and stepped out into downtown Rosewood.

The first thing I noticed was a huge sign on the building next to me that Reid stepped out of last night. Reid's Diner. So he really meant it when he said he lived next door. Never in high school would I have guessed he would start a business when he grew up, much less own a diner. Maybe Rosewood did have a few surprises.

To be honest, I fully expected Reid to try out for a volleyball career like his brother. Even though I left the sport behind in high school, I still watched major games when I could. I saw Ashton Reid playing in the last Olympics, which made me wonder what the Reid brother that I used to know was up to.

Turns out he was opening his own diner. From all of our early morning practices in school, we had quite a rivalry and often stayed late to one up each other. If I ran five miles before practice, he was going to run six the next morning. When he was determined to perfect his jump serve, I made sure to practice on off hours and nailed it before he did.

I turned to walk away from the cafe and walked along the sidewalk to check out the rest of the shops around us. Eight stores down, and everything else remained exactly the same as I remembered it. The florist, bike shop, and theater all could have been pulled straight from a picture ten years ago.

The faint hint of salty sea air from the ocean that was nearby filled my lungs, and a few people passed by me as I walked. Out of habit I scanned their faces to see if they looked familiar, but I wouldn't expect many people to recognize me, except for Reid anyway. When I lived here in high school I didn't exactly make many friends.

As I turned onto another street, I couldn't help but notice how dreamlike this felt. People living their everyday lives went right by me. A woman with her dog who had probably taken this route every day for the past few years the dog had lived. And now here I was to walk past her. In Rosewood.

Tightness claimed my chest while I continued walking further. My pace was too slow. It felt like walking in quicksand or trying to run in a dream. I took a second to stand still and tilted my head back to breathe in the cool breeze.

Two people started chatting around the corner. They sounded friendly, and something about that made my chest feel even tighter. I spun around on my heel and made a beeline to return right back where I came from.

Minutes later, I was out of breath from speed walking. I swung the unlocked door of the cafe open and locked it behind me. The windows were huge, so I took a few more steps and slid down to sit behind a counter for cover.

My breathing was out of control. My heart felt like it was going to burst out of my chest. This wasn't my city. Just forty eight hours ago I was sharing greasy food truck chicken with the man I was going to marry. Everything was set in stone. Stable. For once, everything was just the way I liked it.

I had a long term partner of four years. The job I worked wasn't miserable, and it paid well enough for me to never worry about what my next meal would be or how to pay my rent. My new apartment was in the perfect part of town near the coffee shop I loved most. I was comfortable, safe even.

And now here I was having a panic attack on the floor of my dead grandmother's cafe in a town I fled over ten years ago. Awful, desperate sounds escaped me as I gasped for air. My head hung between my knees, and my hand clutched at my chest, hoping that rubbing my heart would fix it. I had no idea how long I stayed that way.

The thing that finally brought me fully out of it was a knock on the front door that I was hiding from. At least my breathing had evened out mostly at that point. My hands swiped tears from my face and I took a deep breath to focus. I would worry about what the hell caused all of that later.

I grabbed a bag of coffee grounds as I stood up from behind the counter and looked to see none other than Nicholas Reid at my door.

4

Nick

All morning after my encounter with Kelsey I couldn't stop thinking about the girl next door. Literally. Fox was in the very building next to mine and I couldn't help but wonder why. At one point I walked outside to make sure it wasn't all a dream, but a bright blue car stared back at me in the alley behind our shops, and there was no one else it could belong to.

I overcooked a regular's eggs because I got distracted contemplating excuses to go over there and check on her. Pancake batter spilled on the counter as I wondered about how long she would stay in town. She could be planning on leaving today and I would potentially never see her again.

That thought got my ass moving. I left my chef and server alone for a bit and told them I needed to run an errand. After rummaging through files in my office I found the mail I was looking for.

Through the storefront window, the long closed coffee shop looked the same as when I last left it. I took my chances, and knocked as loud as I could without alarming people passing by. Seconds later, a familiar head popped up behind the counter and turned to look at me.

Her cheeks were puffy. Even through the tinted window I could see her eyes were red. She gave me a small grimace and walked around the counter to open the door for me. Her tall frame stood in the doorway blocking me from coming in.

"Two run-ins in less than twelve hours. To what do I owe this pleasure?" She sassed.

I sighed and ran a hand through my hair. She had definitely been crying, her usually confident smooth voice sounded gritty and strained. My hand held out the mail I found in front of me.

"I believe this belongs to you now. The mail lady just dropped them on the floor, so I didn't want to leave them there." She struggled to take eight months' worth of envelopes into both of her hands.

Her eyes looked back up to mine hesitantly. "Have you been cleaning the place too?"

I wasn't expecting her to notice that. I didn't go out of my way to keep it squeaky clean every day, but I checked to make sure the place was in order every few weeks. Evangeline was a nice lady, and there was no way I was going to leave her beloved cafe deserted.

"I clean up the place every now and again when I can." My eyes fell to my sneakers. "So what are you planning on doing with it?"

Her gaze hardened at that and she moved to close the door. "You'll be the first to know. Thanks for stopping by."

Before I could ask again the door was shut and locked. She made an adorable gesture to shoo me away with a pout on her lips. It sounded like she herself didn't know what she was doing with the place. If that was true, I would damn well make an effort to make sure she stayed for as long as possible.

Back in the diner I was met with my twin Ashton and his daughter Ruth sitting at my bar. Ash looked at me with a raised eyebrow. "Where were you?"

I turned to Ruth who was my niece, and by far my favorite person on this Earth. "What do you want for breakfast today Ruthie? French toast?"

A blonde ponytail bobbed on her head as she nodded. "With the strawberry hearts please."

"No roses today?" Her head shook as a response. At six years old she knew exactly what she did and didn't want, and I wouldn't have it any other way.

I moved to the side to start cutting strawberries into the little hearts that she loved. Ashton slid over closer to me, even though I had done my best to avoid his questioning.

"Good morning to you, too. I'll take some eggs and bacon please." I rolled my eyes. My crew knew Ashton and Ruth's orders by heart. The second they walked into the place my cook likely had already started their food.

He paused, but continued talking when he realized I wouldn't respond. "I saw you talking to someone next door." Another pause. "You know Georgia's still really sad about them closing. Is someone buying the place?"

Georgia was Ashton's soon-to-be fiance. She moved to town over a year ago and the two had practically been inseparable ever since. Well more like the three of them, since Ruth was definitely a part of that package deal. They were dating for about a year when he asked me to tag along to go find the perfect ring last month.

I sighed and stopped cutting to stare at my brother. "I have no idea. That's why I walked over there."

"And what did they say?"

"That I would be the first one to know what they were doing with the place."

Ashton's eyes narrowed. "Why are you being so short? Someone piss in your cheerios this morning?"

I finished up the last strawberry heart and turned to wash my hands. Over my shoulder I answered, "No, just curious to see what happens to the place."

"If that's what you say, brother." He walked over to sit back down next to Ruth and I took my time getting their food and bringing it over.

Tension crept into my shoulders while I continued working. I didn't understand why I was feeling so on edge today. My heart was racing after talking to Charlotte, which as an athlete, made no sense considering I hadn't even broken into a sprint.

After dropping off my family's plates, I made myself busy for a bit while they began eating. Returning behind the counter when I ran out of things to do, I looked over at Ruth. "What are you two up to today?"

She smiled brightly with strawberries stuck in her teeth. "We are making popsicles and taking them to the beach. Can you come with us?"

Usually I would make time to hang out with my niece if possible, but there was something in the back of my mind telling me to stay in town today. What if Charlotte needed help with something? I had been waiting months for her to come and she was finally here.

"Not today, Ruthie. The diner's been really busy, so I have extra work to do." Her little face turned into a frown. "No need to worry, though. We still have our weekly ice cream date coming up."

She cheered up a little at that, and I got back to work. Both my brother and niece said bye before they left and Ashton made sure to give me a hard slap on the shoulder. "Good luck with whatever's on your mind, man."

I brushed him off, but I really would need luck. The rest of my shift was smooth as my mind continued to rage on with ways to see Charlotte again. I knew virtually nothing about her life other than she played volleyball in high school, and the dumb details my puppy dog crush forced me to remember. She liked reading, wrote only in pen, and always ate ice cream with weird toppings. Then again, all of that could have changed in the last ten years.

This Charlotte Fox could be a different person to the one I used to know, and she still took the entirety of my attention all day. I sent my chef, Jace, home early to go spend some time with his wife, so I could cook as a distraction.

A busy dinner rush was exactly what I needed. A few hours, dozens of meals, and hundreds of dollars later made my mind much calmer. After closing up shop with my crew and sending them home with leftovers, I went upstairs to catch up on some much needed sleep.

Four days went by, and I saw nothing of my new neighbor. The only thing confirming she was still here was her car parked outside. Every morning and night I found myself checking that it still sat in the back alley while taking out trash.

On the fifth day I woke up to banging. Running a diner meant that I inherently had to be an early riser. My shop opened at six which meant I was up and going at five, and yet this banging still woke me up before my clock went off at five

AM.

I laid in bed listening before getting up to investigate. It was definitely coming from next door. The banging stopped, and I huffed before rubbing a hand over my face and heading back up to bed. What the hell was she doing?

At five I heard more banging, but it stopped again before I got up the nerve to go over there. It was before sunrise. What on earth could she be doing? Did she need help? What if she was trapped somewhere and was banging on the wall for help? I did tell her to knock on the wall if she ever needed anything.

The third time I heard banging I was standing in front of her store in seconds. Through the windows, I saw her sitting on the floor with a hammer in hand and huge pieces of wood laying all around her. I knocked on the door until her head turned to look at me.

Charlotte set down the wood and hammer she was holding to unlock and swing the front door open just enough to speak to me. "Yes?" she said with a hand on her hip. Her expression looked determined, and she radiated more confidence today than the last time I saw her.

"What's with all of the noise? I'm trying to run a business next door." If anything, I was grateful for the excuse to talk to her. But she would only turn me away if I told her that.

She shifted to the side and gestured to the wooden planks behind her. "I'm building shelves. And I too, am trying to run a business here." With the last sentence her lips widened into a beautiful, proud smile.

"Do you need to get your head checked? No one is in here. Let me in. I can help with this." I squeezed past her standing in the doorway and walked into the shop to see one already built bookshelf. I turned back to her. "You built this on your own?"

She rolled her eyes. "What, like it's hard?" I raised an eyebrow. "It was a reference, you won't get it. Obviously I built it. Do you see any helpers standing around?"

I bent down to the one she was currently working on. "These are at least three times your weight. Let me help, this wood is heavy." I picked up the instructions she was reading and started where she left off.

Her loud sigh of frustration made my head turn to look up at her. "Don't you have a business to run?" she said with exasperation.

"It'll be fine. If I leave you to do this alone you'll be banging for the rest of the day," I answered.

"Misogynist," she muttered.

My head jolted up to get a good look at her expression. When I found her smiling at me, I let out a breath of relief. "For the record, that's because two pairs of hands are better than one. Not because you're a woman."

She laughed and sat down next to me with surprisingly no other arguments. Either she really needed help or there was something I was missing. We worked together quietly for a few minutes. I hammered and she used the allen wrench when necessary.

"So what are these shelves going to be used for?" I started. It seemed like the safest question out of all the ones running through my mind.

"Books." I openly glared at her until she continued. "I'm thinking about reopening the shop and having it be a bookstore and cafe. It seems stupid to run just a coffee shop right next door to a diner. And Rosewood needs a bookstore."

My heart pounded at the admission. This meant she was

planning on staying. "It does need a bookstore. And you've got plenty of space for it."

She nodded as she continued screwing in a corner to the bookshelf. "So you don't think it's a dumb idea?"

I hesitated. "Of course not. Do you?"

She stopped screwing to stare at me. "No, but do you think other people will? I doubt anyone in this town remembers me, so what if they just don't show up? Evangeline knew almost everyone that came in."

"They'll come. It's Rosewood, half the town will come just because they're nosey enough to meet the person opening the place. That's what happened with my diner." I tried my best to sound reassuring. Hell, I would bribe people to come in if it meant she would stay.

She nodded and returned back to her work. "How did that happen anyway?"

"What? The diner?"

"Yeah, the last time I saw you, you were destined to be a volleyball legend. Bound for a college or pro team for sure. I saw Ashton play pro, but what happened with you?"

Her voice was quiet, but it held curiosity. The fact that she wondered about me made me feel a little validated in my constant state of thinking about her lately.

"I decided I didn't want to keep playing other than for fun. I didn't feel the same passion that Ashton felt, but we still have a league that gets together every week to play." I set down the hammer to grab another piece of wood. "I went to culinary school and traveled around for a bit before saving up enough money to buy the diner."

"Culinary school?" Her eyes were wide as she looked up at me.

I snickered and nudged her shoulder with mine. "Yes, didn't think I was capable?"

"No, I just had no idea you'd be interested in that. I'm glad you found another passion though. The diner seems to do well."

"It does, thanks." I looked over her jeans with paint smeared on them, and my gaze trailed up to her silky brown hair in a messy bun with strands falling out in all the right places. "What about you?"

She shoved one of those strands of hair back behind her ear to get a good look at me. "What about me?"

"Well, it's been…" I pretended to count on my fingers "Ten years since I last saw you. What happened in that time?"

Her eyes moved to stare at a blank wall. "A lot. I moved to the city and worked my way up in the corporate world. Got a nice apartment. Saw some things, met some people." Her voice trailed off at the end of her sentence. She looked back down at the screw her hand held before grabbing the next piece of wood to screw in.

"Nice. What was your job?"

"Accounting." She blew out a breath. "Riveting, I know."

I chuckled to ease the tension. Clearly other things had happened that she wasn't interested in sharing right now, so I was willing to let that go. For now.

"I can't picture you in a city. You always struck me as a small town girl, but I'm glad you got to try it out for a while." She shot me a glare for that.

"And why is that?" She placed her hands on her lower back and stretched as she continued to look down.

I blinked while I considered her question. "I guess because you never seemed to interact with new people much. Cities have a lot of people."

"Which means they're much easier to hide in. Small towns require seeing the same people all the time." She explained it like it was common sense.

"Well, either way, I'm glad you're back." Moron. I was a moron for saying that. She gave me a suspicious look and then laughed like I told a joke.

It took us the next couple of hours to completely build two more huge bookshelves. When we finished, I lifted them to stand upright and we moved them to the positions she wanted. I stepped back to take in our handiwork and offered her a high five.

"Thanks for helping." She offered a small smile as she spoke.

I nodded. "Anytime. I mean it. I helped Evangeline with stuff like this a lot."

Maybe if she knew I would do this for other people, she would be more likely to let me help. But if I was being honest, my motivations were entirely about getting to see her more.

She slapped a shelf as if testing to see if it would hold up. "We'll see. I'm probably going to have to order a few more of these."

"Sign me up then." I glanced at the door. "I should be getting back. It's almost time for the before school rush."

We walked to the door and I turned before opening it. "Let me know if you need anything at all, Fox."

She always isolated herself in Rosewood during our high school days, and in the time she had been here I hadn't seen her leave the shop once. Anyone would get lonely staying in a place their dead relative used to live.

"Yeah, okay. If I need someone I'll call a friend or something. There's no need to take pity on the poor new girl in town.

Well, sort of new." Charlotte Fox had friends? My next plan of action was figuring out how the hell to get on that list.

I nodded and waved goodbye before walking back into my diner. My steps slowed while I took my sweet time walking back.

5

Charlotte

It took one day for me to decide my game plan. After taking another walk around Rosewood, I was reminded of one of my biggest disappointments in this town when I lived here before. There was no bookstore.

So I got to work and started researching how to open a bookstore. I still wanted to keep the cafe aspect, but also sell books. The storefront was giant, so there was plenty of space to put up bookshelves and still have a small area left for seating. The shelves were the first thing I ordered.

Putting together furniture on my own seemed like the perfect start to this new chapter of my life. The boxes arrived late one afternoon after I spent the entire day out with Dylan visiting local bookstores in other towns to research how they operate. I even made a connection with one of the owners who gave me her card to call if I ever had questions.

Dyl dropped me back off at the store with the promise that I would give her an official tour of Rosewood sometime soon. I waved as her worse for wear car darted off down the street, and walked into the shop to find a bunch of heavy cardboard boxes sitting outside my front door.

Just the act of lifting and moving each box into the store tired me out to the point of exhaustion. I sat and stared at the wall of boxes for a few minutes before deciding to go take a shower and head to bed. The cold water made me feel lighter, and seemed to wash away more and more of my stress with every day I spent here.

I woke up at four the next morning on my painfully stiff couch. I couldn't fall back asleep, so I went ahead and started building. Figuring out the stupid instructions took an hour, but I finally had the first shelf finished around the time Reid showed up.

He stayed, and we built the next two shelves together much quicker than I built the first one on my own. I also got to satisfy my own curiosity about Reid. In the time I lived far away from this small town, I did wonder occasionally how the town and people in it were doing. Mostly Reid and Evangeline since they were the only two people I made a slight connection with when I lived here.

I was glad to know that Reid was happy with what he was doing. He always did seem like the impulsive type, not only did he play volleyball in school, but I remembered him trying out a bunch of other sports just to prove he could do it. The idea that he traveled and fell into a new profession made more sense than him staying right on a straight and narrow path his whole life.

After the shelves were built, I spent the next few days ordering books. I made quite a few phone calls to my new friend Gladys who helped me figure out which books to buy and how many of each to get. The internet and a how-to book for dummies were my other partners in this insane operation.

As I worked to get everything set up to reopen the new bookstore cafe, something kept nagging at the back of my mind. This was a small town, and people had no clue who I was other than a teenager who crashed on her grandmother's couch for a few years. Evangeline had relationships with most of her customers, and they genuinely seemed to enjoy coming to the shop to visit her. That was a quality I was severely lacking in.

The business also needed a name, so I started brainstorming new ideas for what to call the place. It was previously named the 'Rosewood Cafe', and while I wanted to keep aspects of Evangeline in the business, it could use a bit of a refresh in the marketing department. It came to me while I was drinking coffee and flipping through her old romance books. Brewing Pages.

With the hard stuff out of the way, I decided I should get out and hopefully make some friends around town. I strolled around at the park for about twenty minutes when I realized how dumb my plan was. Walking up to people who were enjoying their days, and introducing myself, was too awkward for me to force myself to do. So, I ended up walking back to the shop, but stopped in front of the diner next door instead.

I pushed open the door to Reid's and walked up to the counter to sit down. It wasn't dinner time yet, so the place was pretty quiet. To my right a few seats sat a small girl in a bar stool like mine that definitely required assistance for her to sit in.

Reid walked around the corner a few seconds later. "Okay, Ruthie. I'm ready to go are you-"

He stopped in his tracks as his gaze landed on me. He looked back to the girl, as if double checking that she saw me sitting here too. I laughed at his awkward stance and looked back down at the menu sitting in front of me.

"Fox." He started.

I smiled at his confusion. He stood frozen, like I was a ghost that would scream 'boo' in his face at any second. "Reid."

"What are you doing here?" Oh, shit. Did he not want me here? He seemed friendly enough when he helped me the other day, so I assumed it wouldn't be weird to come in. It wasn't like I came only to see him. I was genuinely hungry too.

I tapped at the menu sitting on the countertop. "Coffee. Food. I hear those are things diners typically serve to people?" My head tilted, testing to see his reaction.

His head shook to wake himself up from this nightmare. A hand ran through his hair and he let out a breath. "Right, of course. What do you want?"

I looked him up and down. His shoulders had broadened a lot since high school. He was wearing his usual black t-shirt that stretched tight across his chest, and a black cap sat on his head.

My hands folded under my chin and I asked sweetly, "Chocolate chip pancakes, please."

He nodded and headed back to the kitchen to call out my order to a chef. The girl next to me turned and asked who I was. She was adorable with her dirty blonde hair in braids and a green dress with polka dots.

"I'm Charlotte. What's your name?"

I wanted to meet people today, and what a perfect opportunity to practice with a kid. She seemed eager to chat with someone while she waited. "I'm Ruth Reid. And I'm going to be in first grade when summer is over."

Her smile was big as she proudly held one finger up. It took a couple seconds for me to process the fact that she said her name was Ruth *Reid*. As in *Reid's* diner. Or also Nicholas *Reid*. Holy shit, did Reid have a kid?

I clearly hadn't asked enough questions the other day when he came over. He mentioned going to culinary school and traveling, but definitely nothing about having a child. Reid walked back to the opposite side of the counter as I felt my brain imploding.

He stood for a moment, and I couldn't help but swivel my head back and forth between them. The dirty blonde hair that Reid had in high school? Check. Perfect cheekbones with a ski slope nose bridge to compliment them? Check. Dark eyes that were the warmest shade of brown? Check. Holy shit, Reid had a kid.

Ruth broke the silence as I continued through my checklist and tried to do the math on how old she was. "Do you know Charlotte? You keep staring at her," she asked Reid.

I looked down and squeezed my eyes tightly to keep from laughing. He awkwardly nodded and cleared his throat. "Yes, we went to school together, she used to play volleyball too."

"Okay, can we go get ice cream now?" Ruth asked eagerly.

Reid nodded and looked back at me. "Do you want to come with us?" He paused, and looked back to the kitchen as if remembering I just ordered food. "You like ice cream, right? We can come back and I'll cook you a real dinner after."

"Pancakes are a real dinner." I defended. He just rolled his eyes and called out to cancel the pancakes.

I sighed with a smile still on my face and stood up. At least I was making some progress on getting out and meeting people in Rosewood. Reid knew plenty of people since he'd lived here nearly his entire life, so maybe he could help me out. And I needed more answers on how the hell he had a kid.

Ruth grabbed Reid's hand after he helped her jump down from the barstool. He leaned down and quietly asked her if she was okay with me joining them, and she nodded shyly. I pretended to be interested in my dirty tennis shoes while I eavesdropped on their cute interaction.

Reid stood up to his full height once they were finished and the two led the way with me trailing behind. The ice cream shop was a few blocks over from us, so it was easier to walk. Ruth walked in the middle with Reid walking closest to the street.

He looked over at me. "Do you still like trail mix in your ice cream?"

"It's called rocky road, and yes, of course I do." I huffed. How the hell did he remember that in the first place? It's not like we were friends when I lived here. I couldn't remember a time we had ice cream together.

I tilted my head down to look at Ruth. "What kind do you like?"

"Bubblegum or cotton candy," she said matter of factly. I did my best to hide my scrunched up nose, but Reid laughed at my reaction anyway.

Once we got to the shop, we each picked out our flavors and Reid paid. I couldn't help but notice that he got coffee flavored ice cream, and something about that made my heart tighten.

We sat down at a table outside and I turned to Ruth again. Getting answers from the kid seemed much more likely than her stoic father. "So, are you excited for first grade?"

She nodded excitedly. "My new teacher has candy in the room and Mallory will be in my class this year."

I share an impressed look with Reid. "That sounds very exciting."

"Mhm, so what do you do?" This kid asked me like she was a full grown adult that had been participating in small talk for at least twenty years.

"Well, I was an accountant, but now I'm opening a bookstore and cafe next to the diner."

"The place where the nice old lady used to work?"

I nodded. "Yeah, she was my grandmother."

Ruth dug out another bite of ice cream with her spoon. It smeared messily along her cheek as she missed her mouth a little before she kept talking. "She told my daddy that he should marry Georgia. I think he should too, but he still hasn't yet."

My head snapped to shoot Reid a confused stare. He was in a relationship too? I figured after more than a week of living next door I would have seen a woman, but then again I just found out he had a kid.

Reid mussed Ruth's hair and responded for me, "One day, kid. You've just gotta be patient."

I suddenly felt very uncomfortable in my seat. If there was a woman he was planning on marrying, why wasn't she here? He must have noticed my tension, because he caught my gaze as I was processing even more information. My cheeks felt hot and my clothes were suddenly too tight. This reaction was totally uncalled for, it made sense that his life had changed a lot since I last saw him.

Before I could continue processing that thought, I was caught off guard by a shriek. "Daddy!"

I followed Ruth's line of sight and suddenly a lot of puzzle pieces clicked together all at once. Walking toward us was

Ashton Reid, Nick's twin brother. Ruth shot out of her seat to run up to him and he spun her in a big bear hug.

Reid twisted in his seat and I caught his grimace before he schooled his face again. "You're early."

Ashton gave his brother a huge smile while walking Ruth back to her chair. "Nice to see you too, brother. Practice let out early, so I figured I'd come join you two."

Then Ashton turned to me. He paused as if he recognized me, but couldn't quite put a name to the face. His eyes squinted and I gave him a few seconds to remember. "Charlotte Fox."

I smiled, relieved that I didn't have to remind him of my name. "Ashton Reid, I'm honored the famous Olympian remembers little ol' me."

He laughed and took a seat across from me. "If I remember correctly, you were close to volleyball royalty yourself back in high school. What are you doing back in town? I thought you hightailed it out of here a long time ago."

Reid shot me a glance. I chose my answer carefully. "My grandmother died, so I'm taking over her shop."

Ashton looked to Reid, confused. Reid clarified for me. "Her grandmother is Evangeline, the woman that owned the cafe."

Ashton's eyebrows raised almost comically. "No way." He locked eyes with me again. "How did I not know that? I'm sorry for your loss."

I grimaced. That phrase was going to take some getting used to. Since I hadn't come back to Rosewood after her death, I never really had anyone to talk to about her. "It's okay, we weren't super close."

Ashton nodded and turned back to his daughter. "Saving a little extra for later, honey bee?" He grabbed a napkin and wiped her face from cheek to cheek.

She giggled and I found myself smiling at the sweet interaction. Reid caught my gaze when I felt him staring at me, so I turned back to my ice cream.

Our dessert was all eaten within minutes. The local Rosewood ice cream shop made their own ice cream in house, and it was practically a delicacy. I relished in the familiar taste and scarfed it down faster than I should have.

I set down my empty cup and looked around when a memory hit me. Reid and I did get ice cream together once, he lost a bet that the girl's team would get further than the boy's team in our high school state championship. He had to buy me ice cream as my reward, but did he really remember what kind I liked after all this time?

We all stood up to leave and Ashton said goodbye first. "I can drop you both off, if you want? We've got to get to bed since she has swim practice in the morning."

Reid and I shared a look and I let him answer. "We'll just walk back, it's not far."

We both waved goodbye to the truck as they drove off. Reid turned to me with a hint of amusement on his face. "Did you think Ruth was my kid?"

I kept my head facing the sidewalk in front of us. "She does happen to share a last name and look a lot like you."

He openly laughed at that and I just rolled my eyes while staring at the ground. A smile snuck its way onto my face. The sound of his laugh was music to my ears that I didn't expect to like.

"I don't have any kids. We probably should have been more thorough when sharing about ourselves." He breathed out after calming down his laugh.

Then he turned to me with a more serious face. "Do you?"

I shook my head quickly. "None that I know of." He snorted at my dumb joke. "Are you in a relationship? Or is Georgia someone your brother is seeing?"

The questions came out before I could even think about how it would sound. He looked over at me through his pretty eyelashes.

"No, I'm single. Georgia is Ashton's girl." He paused and the debate was clear on his face. Finally, he asked the question anyway. "I'm guessing there aren't any men hiding out in the trunk of your cute little car?"

I let out a self pitying laugh. "Hell no. No relationships for me."

We walked the rest of the way home in silence. I wondered if he was thinking about me or his past relationships. I glanced over to see if I could tell from the look on his face, but as usual, Reid had the best poker face.

The fact that he invited me to spend time with him and his niece felt like it should mean something. He went out of his way twice now to help me out. Both when I was trapped outside of the shop that first night in town, and when he caught me building giant shelves on my own. As I looked over at him again to decode his intentions, it struck me that he could totally be friending me out of pity.

He had been overly helpful, and mentioned several times how close he was with my grandmother. Which made me wonder if she ever told him about me. Not that she knew a whole lot more than he did in the first place.

I only ever told Evangeline that my mother left home, and I got evicted. She sadly didn't seem surprised about that, and I doubted she would ever share my story with someone else without me knowing. So, Reid had no way of knowing about my shitty mother. Or my shitty ex for that matter.

If he was being nice out of pity I wanted nothing to do with him. I had enough self pity lately with all of the shit I had to deal with, and I had no time for performing in front of someone else to make them feel better.

"What's with the face?" Reid's words pulled me out of my thoughts.

I looked over at him with a frown on my face. "What face?"

"You're making a face like you're trying to solve all of the world's problems on your own. And your hands are tightened into fists. What were you thinking about?"

I forcefully unclenched my hands. "Are you pity-friending me?"

He paused a little mid-step. "What the hell does that mean?"

"You know, being my friend because you pity me. Sounds self explanatory to me." I stopped walking to openly interrogate him while fully facing him.

His annoyed face made me believe I was partially right. He laughed with disbelief coloring his face before reasoning with me, "Fox, if you think I need to pity you to be your friend, maybe you should go talk to a professional."

"Why did you invite me out tonight then?" I wondered.

He sighed and looked down the street as if he would rather be anywhere else right now. "Maybe I like talking to you."

I openly laughed at that. A cruel laugh that made me bend over to catch my breath. I pushed my hair back out of my face as I rose back to my full height. No man had ever gone out of their way to spend time with me because they 'liked talking to me' not even my ex fiance.

He waited for me to finish laughing and stared at me with those dark eyes. He quietly added, "It's true. I'm not being

48

funny."

I exhaled and patted him on the shoulder before we kept walking. "Nice try, Reid. Don't worry, I'll figure it out eventually. Everyone always shows their true colors in the end," I joked.

This time he turned to face me. "You think I'm hanging out with you for some ulterior motive?"

I just shrugged. "I guess. Isn't that why anyone makes a friend?"

I thought about my sentence for a while after speaking. Dylan and I became friends out of a shitty serving job. We bonded over the hellish work place we shared, and even after we both quit and walked out together, our friendship lasted years after that. I had other friends in my life, but none that lasted longer than the situation deemed the relationship convenient.

Maybe that's what Reid was trying to do. Make nice, since we would be living right next to each other. It would be a friendship of convenience, and I supposed that made enough sense to satisfy me for now.

Reid grumbled something and clenched his jaw. When we reached his diner I kept walking toward my cafe, but he stopped me with a gentle hand on my arm. "I promised you dinner."

I had totally forgotten about that. "Oh, are you sure?" He really did not look like he wanted me around any longer than necessary.

"I'm sure, come on." He kept his hand on the back of my arm near my shoulder and led me through the busy restaurant and past the kitchen. I gave him a confused look, but he paid me no mind.

We walked up the stairs to his loft apartment and I took in the layout. It looked a lot like mine, but he actually furnished the place, so it had a comfortable living space and not just a desk with room for storage. Which reminded me, I still needed to buy a bed.

Out of the corner of my eye, I caught Reid's bed tucked away in the one private corner of his loft. His bed was made and the dark bedding perfectly matched the black clothes he always wore. There were decorations all around with pictures and various souvenirs, but it felt too intrusive to go out of my way to inspect all of them. His living room consisted of even more trinkets and a flat screen mounted on the red brick wall that our buildings shared. He even had a warm plush red rug tucked under his coffee table that tied it all together.

His eyes met mine and he gestured for me to sit down on his leather couch. It was an open floor plan, so the couch was close enough to the kitchen for me to see exactly what he was doing. I sat quietly and let him work without any further questions.

6

Nick

Never in my life had I felt so on edge while cooking. Somehow, Fox had it in her head that I pitied her, and that was why I kept wanting to see her. For someone so smart, she could be a little dense sometimes.

I decided to make her one of my comfort recipes that everyone loved. A nice bowl of shrimp and grits did a lot to ease the mind. And thankfully, I had a full restaurant of ingredients downstairs to make it exactly the way I like.

She sat quietly on my couch, and every time I looked over she was watching me cook. I should probably say something, she looked awkward perched at the end of my couch with a stiff back. Which reminded me, had she bought a bed yet?

"So have you ordered a bed yet, or are you still sleeping on a twenty year old couch every night?" My words came out harsher than I intended.

She let out a cute little laugh at my awkwardness. "My back will never recover. I've honestly considered sleeping on the hardwood; it might be a little comfier."

I cringed, thinking about having to sleep on that couch every night. It had been over a week since she was in town, and just one night on it was enough to do damage. I sighed while thinking of a way to offer my help without offending her. The problem was that I didn't want her to think I was trying to help her out of pity again.

I turned to face her while still stirring the grits as they cooked. "Do you need money for a mattress? Or if you need help getting it to your place, my brother has a truck I can borrow."

Her face immediately tensed and her eyes narrowed. "I have money, Reid. You really think I'm some poor charity case don't you?"

I turned back to my food and thought over my next words carefully. Help was taboo in Charlotte Fox's world, but I was determined to break her rules anyway. At least that was one thing that hadn't changed since I knew her before. Stubbornness was a key component of what made her who she was.

The only thing that seemed to work with her was being completely honest. So I tried my best at that without giving away the fact that she ran through my mind damn near every second of every day since she came back to town.

"No, I think you're stubborn as fuck and you don't know when to ask for help. You're clearly alone here, and it bothers me that you're sleeping on a shitty couch every night when I could just help you fix it." I turned to meet her eyes. "Really, it would only take a few hours. So what do you need? Money or a ride? Or both." I added for good measure.

She sighed. "I honestly don't really need either. I sort of pushed that task to the side in all of the chaos of trying to put together a bookstore on top of reminding myself how to run

52

a cafe." I stayed quiet in hope that she would continue. "A ride would be nice though, if it's not a huge hassle."

A breakthrough. She actually accepted my offer of help. I looked through one of my tall windows to make sure pigs weren't flying around out there.

Then I turned to her and forced my words to stay even, although I was secretly stoked on the inside. I honestly expected trying to be her friend would be more difficult than this, but maybe she really had changed since I last knew her. We were no longer just two kids trying to one up each other on a volleyball court.

"Sure, just let me know when. Ash is home most days before four, so anytime before that is probably good." I turned off the burner and set the grits to the side. Then I started working on cleaning shrimp.

"Thanks, Reid." I heard Charlotte mutter from behind me.

I glanced over my shoulder and saw her facing away from me staring at the blank TV. "Anytime, Fox. Now, do me a favor and turn something on. You're awfully grumpy when you're hungry."

She turned and glared at me after snatching the remote off of the table. "And here I thought you 'enjoyed talking to me'," she mocked.

I smiled down at the shrimp my hands were busy with, so she couldn't see the dopey grin on my face. I absolutely loved that smart ass mouth. The thought of getting to argue with her more put me in an even better mood.

By the time our meal was ready, Fox was fully turned around on the couch, peering over the back of it at me like a cat I had forgotten to feed. I met her eyes with both of our plates in hand and tilted my head to the small dining table I had in the corner. She jumped up from the couch and sat down in a chair quickly.

"It smells amazing," she offered. I couldn't hold back the smile this time as I set the plate down in front of her.

"Thanks, Fox. Now get to eating before you start interrogating me again." Her eyes rolled at my order, but she obeyed anyway. I waited to witness her first bite in action and her eyes rolled for an entirely new reason this time. A cocky smirk found its way to my face.

She tried her best to flatten her face, but a small smile still stayed there. "It's good. You made a good decision to go to culinary school."

I almost fell over in my chair at the compliment. She giggled as I clutched my chest dramatically. "From you, Fox? That means the world." I said with sarcasm laced in the words, but I truly did mean it.

We ate the rest of dinner in silence that was only interrupted by her happy hums, and I relished the satisfied smile on her face as she finished her plate. She must have really been hungry because I caught her doing a cute little happy wiggle a few times. After she finished, she waited for me to clear my last few bites.

She stood up to grab both of our plates and brought them over to my sink to start washing up. I followed her and stood next to her to see what she was doing. "Woah, woah, woah, Foxy. Guests don't do the dishes."

Especially not guests that I wanted to stay for longer. She brushed me off and continued doing the dishes with that same small smile on her face. I made a mental note to cook for her more often. "You cooked, so I clean. It's only fair."

Arguing with her seemed pointless, so I grabbed the dishes

54

after she rinsed to put them in the dishwasher. "Can you show me how to do that sometime?"

I froze at her question. I would show her how to do damn near anything she wanted. "Didn't you burn a cheese pizza in culinary class back in school and set off a fire alarm?"

"They had us cooking them in a *microwave*! It's not my fault, I thought the instructions said six minutes and not sixty seconds."

I couldn't help but let my shoulders shake as I continued loading dishes into the dishwasher. She shot a disapproving look at my laughter, but I saw her smile a little when she turned back to what she was doing.

"I'll teach you sometime, but first we need to get you a bed." I insisted.

"Yeah, yeah. You're awfully bossy now, you know?" I smiled over at her. Then I purposely let my hand slide across hers as I took the next plate from her.

Her eyes met mine, and I appreciated the dark green that shined back at me. She was absolutely stunning, and looking at her for too long knocked my confidence a little. "I run a business, which requires me to be a bit bossy. At least that's one thing you'll thrive at when you open your shop."

She bumped my hip with hers and I snickered at her scrunched nose. We finished up the rest of the dishes and she sighed. "I should get back now. Thanks for today, it was good to get out."

"Let me know when you can go get that bed." I ordered.

Her eyes rolled again. "I will, dad." We walked down the stairs and I followed her all the way to her back door out in the alley. "I was thinking of opening on September 1st."

The way she spoke made it sound like she was divulging an

exciting secret. I did my best to show that made me happy. "September 1st sounds like the perfect date. I'll definitely be there."

Her head tilted and her nose lifted while she looked me over. "Do you read?"

I scoffed at the question, and she smiled with those pretty eyes shining at me. She was teasing me again. "Sometimes, but I also happen to drink a lot of coffee."

"You have an entire diner which sells coffee." Her finger poked my chest.

I grabbed her hand and pulled her closer with it until we were almost nose to nose. She was addictive, I wanted to be even closer. Our smiles remained on our faces as I leaned in a little more. "It's not the same, Fox. You better save a cup for me on opening day."

She retrieved the hand I was holding like it was singed with flames and backed up to open her door. "I'll see what I can do."

And just like that she was gone.

The next day was Saturday, which meant it was time for volleyball practice. I got ready and headed out to the local gym where we all got together. Most of our group knew each other from high school. Some of the other guys even played pro at some point like my brother. We mostly played for fun, but occasionally did events for crowds like the charity match we did last summer.

I reached the gym earlier than most everyone else, like usual. Nowadays all of my friends were getting old, so some of them had wives and kids to tend to. As I was sitting down on a bench to retie my shoes, a familiar face walked up to me.

I looked up at my long time friend, Will Rose, and gave him a short nod in greeting. He grunted as a response and sat down next to me to switch out his own shoes. Our friendship was perfect because we were both stubborn assholes with demanding jobs that didn't feel the need to fill silence all of the time.

He turned to me after his shoes were tied. "I heard you broke up with Kelsey."

I flinched at the statement. Will was never exactly in the Rosewood gossip mill, so those words coming out of his mouth sounded strange. "Yeah, I did."

"Was it just not working out?" Will Rose was asking me about my love life. What the hell kind of dimension did I wake up in this morning?

"Since when are you the love doctor?" I asked my friend.

He laughed and bent down to grab a water bottle from his bag. "I spend eighteen hours a day at work six days a week, man. I just need to talk about something else for once, and your sudden break up seemed like an easy bet."

"You need a subscription to some cheap reality TV then." He gave me a bored look. I contemplated actually sharing the reason I broke up with Kelsey. If there was anyone I could rely on to react calmly to this it was Will. "Charlotte Fox came back to town."

"Fox. That sounds familiar." I gave him a moment to think. Charlotte knew most of the guys on the team since volleyball practice bled together sometimes for the girls and guys back in school. But she had never really made an effort to be friendly. She was definitely a classified loner, but that was one of the things I loved about her.

Will's head shot up. "Oh, the girl you were obsessed with back in school. She came back to Rosewood? I thought she had family issues or something that she was running from."

"I was not obsessed with her." It was a knee jerk reaction. "And she never liked small town life. She was only here for a few years to go to school."

Will's eyes narrowed at me. "Right. And why is she back in town now?"

"Her grandmother died, did you know Evangeline? She was the owner of the cafe next door to me."

"Yeah, I used to go there every morning. I had no idea they were related."

"Well, when she died she left the shop to Charlotte. I'm not sure what took her so long, but she's back in town and opening the shop again. It's going to sell books now too."

"So you broke up with Kelsey?" He stared at me with an unreadable expression.

I sighed and stared at the volleyball net across the gym. "I knew I had to the same night I saw her back in town." I met Will's stare. "Is that crazy?"

He lightly laughed at me and the corners of his eyes crinkled. "Yeah, man it is. But when you know, you know."

I raised an eyebrow at his answer. "Are you planning on telling everyone about this when practice starts?"

"That would be your brother's job." He stood up and slapped me on the shoulder. "Your secret's safe with me though. I'll never need a reality TV subscription in Rosewood."

The rest of the team showed up with varying degrees of lateness. We warmed up and played practice games for a few hours. My brother made an effort to nag me about breaking up with Kelsey, but I did my best to brush him off. Apparently our break up was not as quiet as I thought, because the whole town heard about Kelsey walking into my diner and out of my life.

I still didn't tell Ash about Charlotte. He questioned my reasoning for breaking up with Kelsey, and I would bet all of my stars that the ever perceptive Ruth mentioned my staring at Fox during our ice cream date. But thankfully, my brother gave up on trying to talk about it after a few hours.

7

Charlotte

Three weeks later, I was unboxing one of my last book shipments. It felt surreal after rushing to prepare these last few weeks that the store would actually have customers in a month or so. A few weeks ago, the thought of running this shop made me sick to my stomach, but now I felt much lighter, like I was finally on the right path.

I had only one big book delivery left before I had enough stock to open. The opening date was set and my bookshelves were mostly full. On the cafe side, I had a food truck delivery due for a week before opening with all of the coffee, cups, and additives I could possibly need. That part was much less stressful thanks to my past experience helping Evangeline order the truck.

Through the store front windows I saw people walk past and point at the huge banner hanging up. They excitedly chatted as they walked past and I hoped it meant they would show up on opening day. I had this strange recurring nightmare that I would dramatically turn the closed sign over to show that we were open and not a single person would show. My therapist said it could reflect my inner insecurities about being neglected, but it seemed like a very real possibility.

If I had one sense of comfort, it was that I knew Reid would show up. Over the past few weeks he also managed to check in and bring me dinner more often than not. His lame excuses ranged from needing to try out new recipes to accidentally cooking more than he needed. The feeling was mutual though, because I found myself hanging around his diner when I missed Dylan and wanted someone to talk to.

I also had him to thank for my satisfying nightlife. Not that we hooked up or anything, but he took me to buy a new bed frame and mattress. I had slept well every night since.

Actually, he always seemed to be around right when I needed someone. He caught me trying to hang up that 'Coming Soon' banner on my own within the first ten minutes of trying. And every time I had a book delivery he was outside helping me move the boxes before I could manage one trip on my own.

Sometimes he even stayed to eat dinner with me when he dropped it off. It was helpful to bounce business ideas off of someone who had experience. My new seventy year old business owner friend, Gladys, was helpful, but Reid was a bit more relatable. He built his diner from the ground up in a town that wasn't used to change.

My phone ringing on the counter showed that Dylan was calling. She was supposed to make a trip down here last week to finally see Rosewood, but got a callback for a job. The girl really needed to pay her rent, so I assured her we could do the small town tour another time.

"Hey, Dyl. What's up?"

"I got it! You are speaking to the new regional manager of

Ducky's Ice Cream," she proudly bragged.

"Holy shit. Someone trusted *you* to be a regional manager? You've gotta put me in contact with your interview coach."

"Why would you need interview coaching? You have your very own business, boss lady."

"I need to do research on who *not* to hire when I finally get around to looking for employees," I said.

"Ha ha. Very funny. Now congratulate me please. This is an impressive thing that I've pulled off!" she whined.

"Great job, Dyl. You're going to do great work managing the ice cream makers of today's generation."

She laughed and sighed softly. "So, how is the cutest bookstore on planet Earth going?"

"Great, I managed to pull it off somehow. Seems like we're both impressive con artists. I'm guessing the new job means you can't make it for opening?"

She huffed. "No, there isn't any vacation time for at least three months. But I will totally quit if you want me there." I laughed at her offer. "And you're not a con artist if you actually have the skills to back up the job position."

I rolled my eyes and started straightening up coffee bags below the counter with the phone held between my ear and shoulder. "Please do not quit. It's a great opportunity, maybe this will finally be the job that can hold down Dylan Chase."

She scoffed. "Yeah, right." Dylan was quiet for a moment before continuing. "So how is therapy going?"

Therapy was something I started in the last few weeks. Starting a business on my own forced me to be alone with my thoughts a lot. In the past, I dealt with my issues by throwing myself into work until whatever was bothering me turned into indifference. But even working on the bookstore wasn't enough to distract me this time.

So I decided I was overdue for trying out therapy. It was going well so far, even though it felt very strange to blurt out my sad little life story to this poor unsuspecting therapist. He wanted to focus on things like my mom leaving and my grandmother dying at first. I tried my best to explain to him that the past was the past and I was totally over my old wounds. I just wanted help with these damn panic attacks.

My therapist insisted that it was all connected. We can't just organize our past trauma into a neat little shelf and forget about it. I disagreed, but I went along with his plan anyway and we started at the beginning. Twice a week and six sessions later, we had already worked ourselves up to my fiance cheating on me.

Talking about my mother was something I had never done with anyone. I might have mentioned her habit of disappearing to Evangeline when we first met, or joked about it with Dylan, but that was about it. It felt uncomfortable to try and remember all of the things that happened. But once I walked out of that therapy office I had to admit I felt a little less pressure.

"Therapy is fine. We talked about the asshole in my last session."

"Good, you sound happier lately. It seems to be working well for you," she said thoughtfully.

"Well enough." While I had opened up to my therapist, it still felt weird to talk about going to therapy with anyone else.

I glanced at the darkening sky outside and sighed. Moving to Rosewood had clearly been the best choice, but I did miss seeing Dylan. She was my best friend and phone calls weren't the same.

"What if I come to you sometime? We can hang out after work one day," I offered.

Dylan gasped obnoxiously. "Charlotte Fox, do you miss me?" Her annoyingly big smile was audible even through the phone.

"We're best friends. I believe that would be normal." I ground out even though a smile pulled at my own lips.

"Any time, Char. You could drive down here tomorrow and I would make myself readily available."

I laughed at her eagerness. "I don't know about tomorrow, but sometime soon. We'll see how this week of setting up the store goes and I'll decide then if I can spare a day away."

A mail truck pulling up outside caught my attention. That must be the last delivery that I've been waiting for. "Hey, Dyl. I've gotta go, my last set of books are being delivered."

"Okay, but fair warning, I'm going to need a full play by play of everything I'm missing. So make sure to memorize every second of it for me. Oh, and take notes if you need to. I'm talking down to each and every book you've bought and the set up of the store and-"

I pulled my phone away from my ear as she continued to ramble on. "Okay, Dyl. Got it. I'll draw you a treasure map too in case you need it. Bye, love you." And with that I hung up.

Strolling outside, I felt the evening breeze wrap around me. It was a quiet Thursday night and there were a few people still walking around town. I took the clipboard my delivery guy handed to me and signed it.

"Thanks, again." I added. This poor man was probably sick and tired of delivering all of my heavy books.

He took his time rolling around the dozen boxes on a cart to my store front. I started carrying the first one inside when

64

the diner owner next door just so happened to appear.

"Reid, I've got this. It's still dinner rush isn't it?"

He ignored me as usual and lifted two boxes. "Do you want these on the table?"

I sighed at him pointedly. Although I secretly enjoyed his overly helpful act. "Yes, please." We continued bringing boxes inside in silence and I waved the delivery man goodbye.

After we finished bringing the last box inside I turned to Reid. "You're going to make a great husband someday, Nicholas. Your ability to show up when needed is uncanny." The comment was meant to be a joke, but lacked my usual sass.

"I make sure to come right on time. Not too early like some other men you might know." His face was dead serious.

I couldn't help but burst out laughing. "Good to know, now shoo. Out of my store please, you have your customers to get back to." I playfully escorted him to the door while sweeping my hands in a shooing motion before holding it open for him.

"Thank you, Reid." I really was grateful for him, after spending a few weeks in Rosewood we were quickly becoming friends.

"Anytime, Fox."

I turned to start unboxing my last delivery. Some of the books in this box were special editions, so I was excited to get them out and display them on the table in the middle of the store. I had an entire plan in my mind of how to organize everything in a pyramid so the display table was nice to look at.

My second box in, I heard a knock at my door. I hadn't locked it behind Reid, so I just called out that he could come in. That man really could not stay away for long.

"Did you forget somethi-" I cut myself off as I turned and

saw who was in front of me.

   Motherfucker.

8

Nick

I managed to get in two visits with Fox today, and I hadn't even brought over dinner yet. This morning she had a large delivery with new tables for the cafe that I helped bring in and set up. Then she had a book delivery in the evening that I helped with. It was a quick visit and I had just walked back in the diner when I felt on edge.

There was no logical reasoning for me to feel uncomfortable. I had literally just seen Charlotte minutes ago, but something in me felt I needed to go back again. My draw to her only got stronger every day and it was getting to the point where it pained me to not see her for longer than a day. I was hopeless.

I tried to push the nagging feeling away and help out my chef who was backed up in the kitchen from the dinner rush. A few minutes later, he was all set up and the hair on the back of my neck still stood up, so I looked over at him and told him I'd be back.

The walk over to her store through the front of mine took less than a minute. I saw it through the window before I burst into the shop. A man that was much taller than she was had Charlotte cornered against a bookshelf and was angrily spitting words in her face.

I had never seen her look more uncomfortable and livid. My legs carried me to them in the blink of an eye and I fisted the back of his shirt to haul him away from her. All I caught of the conversation was him asking her where 'it' was.

"Who the fuck are you?" I asked. My heart felt like it was going to burst from my chest. My hand was clenched so tightly in his shirt it ached, every muscle in my body painfully tensed to hold back my temper.

His lip curled up in a disapproving snarl at me and he took a step back. I begrudgingly let go of his shirt. "I could ask you the same. Who the fuck are you?"

I looked back at Charlotte to make sure she was okay. She looked mortified.

"I'm her fucking man. So tell me, who the fuck are you?" I responded. The need to protect her was only heightened by the adrenaline rush. This guy was going to back the fuck off whether or not he wanted to.

His gaze slid back to Charlotte. "Funny. My ring was on her finger less than a month ago." My heart beat harshly for a new reason now.

Fox stepped up behind my shoulder. "And if I recall correctly your dick was in someone else less than a month ago, too. Get the fuck out. And don't come back here."

The asshole stayed for a minute staring at the both of us before shoving my shoulder and stalking off. I grit my teeth watching him go.

Fox's quiet huff brought me back to reality. "You're my man now?" She quietly asked. She was trying to tease me but it fell flat.

"Are you okay?" She looked taken aback at the question.

"Yeah, I'm fine. I just wasn't expecting him to come here." She curled in on herself and crossed her arms. I couldn't fight back the urge this time as I wrapped my arms around her and held her.

"I'm glad you're okay. Do you want me to kick his ass? Because I can go catch him right now." I pulled back to look at her face.

She chuckled and retreated from my arms. "While I would love to see that, no. He's not worth it anyway."

I wanted to ask more. I had about a million questions running through my mind, but I really didn't want to make her any more uncomfortable than she already was. "What did he want?"

She turned her head to break eye contact. "Nothing, he's just an asshole. I doubt he'll come back after that."

Her doubt was not comforting. "Did you let him in?"

She shook her head. "I thought it was you coming back, so I just called for him to come in."

My fist clenched again. "You need to lock your doors, Fox." She nodded and continued to look at the floor. This unconfident look was not natural on Charlotte.

"Have you eaten yet?" I offered. Her head shook again.

I nodded and pulled out my phone. In a few minutes, I had takeout ordered to be delivered to her shop. She stood still, watching me as I typed. When I was done I put away my phone and nodded to the new table and chairs she bought for her store.

"Go sit and I'll start unboxing these." Her eyes narrowed at me and she remained standing. "Seriously, you should go sit for a minute."

She turned around and quietly went to sit at one of the pretty wooden tables. Half of me wanted her to bite back with her usual sass, but she was clearly feeling vulnerable with the intrusion. I didn't blame her.

We stayed silent for twenty minutes while she watched me, I opened all of the boxes and started stacking books on the center table. A delivery person knocking at the door startled me. When I returned with boxes of noodles and chicken her eyes narrowed on the food like they always did. My girl was definitely a foodie.

As we ate she slowly started to turn back into her usual self. Her hunched over shoulders straightened and her posture opened back up. The crease between her eyebrows faded and her eyes were relaxed as she looked at me.

"Do you have cameras or something in my store?" Her question had me taken aback.

"Cameras in your store?" My eyebrows scrunched together.

"How the hell do you always know when to come over here?"

"Delivery trucks usually have this loud beeping sound when they reverse, so it's pretty easy-" I spoke slowly.

"Okay well how about just now? I don't think that asshole comes with a built-in beeper." She questioned.

I hesitated. While tapping my chopsticks together I debated on lying just so I didn't sound crazy, but one look at Charlotte's face reminded me that I could never lie to her. "I just had a feeling."

"A feeling?" Her eyelids shut halfway as if staring at me hard enough would change my answer.

"Yes." I continued eating my food.

She stopped eating to stare at me. "You had a feeling. That I

70

needed help."

"Yes."

"And you just magically happened to be right?"

"Yes."

She stared for another minute before letting out a final frustrated noise and returned to her food. I had no more understanding of it than she did. We finished our food while I focused on going through what just happened. Maybe I needed to set her up with a security system.

"Thanks for the food." She muttered as I gathered up our trash.

I finished shoving it all in the plastic bag it came in and stood to go put it in her bin. "Of course, now how do you want these? I'm guessing this isn't how you want to leave them for opening day." I gestured to the books that I messily unpacked on the table.

She rose to stand next to me as we looked over the table. She snickered at my work. "You have a real knack for this, Reid."

I rolled my eyes. When it was clear I wasn't leaving until we finished, she pointed to another box of books that I could stack on a shelf in the self-help section.

"So, you were going to marry that guy?" I tried my best to keep my voice casual.

She sighed down at the books she was organizing. "For some inexplicable reason, yes." Her voice paused and then continued. "Actually, I know the reason. It felt safe, we had been in a relationship for years, and while it was boring, there were no glaring issues. So I went along with it."

A box loudly slammed on the table she was working on. "And then I found him cheating on me. I guess love is never really safe. You always run the risk of getting burned."

I stopped what I was doing to stare at her. *"That* guy was cheating on *you?"* Charlotte Fox was lightyears out of that scrub's league. I was shocked that she would even go on a single date with him, much less agree to marry him.

Fox just smiled sadly back at me. I looked to the door and started calculating if I could find the asshole somehow. Maybe my new spidey senses would come in handy.

"Love just isn't my thing I guess. Evangeline would hate me saying that."

"That asshole just isn't your thing. I promise you, Fox, this is a him problem, not a you problem."

Her shoulders shrugged and she continued working. I wanted to go over there and show her how easy it was to love her. How I had pined over her for weeks, and even after ten years of not knowing her it was so easy to fall right back into it.

But this was Charlotte Fox, and she deserved better than some half assed attempt at consoling her. She deserved the best man I could be. Confessing my love for her after just meeting her ex fiance and nearly pummeling him, was not the best I could be.

We finished setting up the rest of the books and Charlotte grabbed signs to spread around the shelves and table. I found a broom and swept, while she finished setting up. When she was finished, she rubbed her palms over her pants and backed up to stand by the front door.

She took in the store and looked satisfied. I moved to stand next to her to get the full effect of the fully stocked book side of the cafe in all of its glory. This was still definitely once Evangeline's cafe, but now Fox had her mark on it too. It was a perfect blend of their two personalities.

"It looks great, Fox. You did great." We shared a look and she smiled before biting her lip. I wanted to pull that full bottom lip between my teeth to celebrate.

"Thanks, I couldn't have done it without you." My eyes rolled at that. She certainly could have done it without me. Charlotte had always done whatever it was she set her mind on.

"Not true, but you're welcome." I smirked. "I'm just the dog that comes when called remember?" She snorted and rolled her eyes.

She continued to bite her lip for a minute while analyzing the store, and I was entranced at the sight. "Do you want the first coffee?"

"The first coffee?"

A playful smirk lit up her face. "Yeah, I couldn't stand not being able to make my own coffee the way I like it. I went to the store earlier to get a small supply to hold me over until the food truck delivery. Come and be my first customer."

I watched her walk around the counter and stand at the register. I took that as my cue to start moving and face her on the opposite side. She plastered a fake cheery smile on her face. "Good morning, what can I get for you today?"

"You know it's literally dark outside right?" I turned to look out the window at the very dark night sky.

Her eyes rolled. "Just go along with it, dummy."

"Good morning, Fox. I'll have my usual please." I waited for her to huff and ask what my usual was, but she turned and got to work without any further questions.

Watching her with a close eye, I realized she was making a latte, which actually was my usual. I had no clue how the hell she would know that, but she did. She continued to work, the milk steamer screeched and her metal spoon clanged around as she mixed in one sugar.

She threw a lid on top and slid the cup over to me gently. "There you are."

"How did you know my usual?" I asked while blowing to cool down the latte.

"It's what you got back in high school, I used to work here all the time remember? Most people stick to their coffee orders for life," she answered confidently.

"And you remembered my coffee order from back in high school?"

She paused for a moment and shrugged before turning to wipe down the counter and put away the milk. "I remember most people's. It says a lot about their personality."

I thought about that for a moment. Mine probably meant I was boring, and couldn't help but indulge a little bit with one sugar added.

"You forgot the most important part though," I said.

She turned her body toward me and looked accusingly at the cup. "What did I forget?"

I pulled my wallet out from my back pocket and held it up for her to see. "I haven't paid."

She slowly blinked at me. "You're not paying."

"I am. Now ring me up, Fox. We have to make sure this thing works." I waved at the register.

"It works. You're not paying, you've brought me dinner practically every night for free."

"This does not set a good expectation for your business. Giving away your first cup for free could be bad luck. What if it's an omen that you won't make any money?"

We held a staring contest before she finally gave in. "Fine, but I am paying the next time I come into the diner."

I nodded even though there was no way in hell I was ever letting her do that. Charlotte Fox didn't know yet that what was mine was hers, but I would pretend to take part in this little game for the time being, if that's what she wanted.

She took my card and swiped it. A receipt printed and we both let goofy smiles take over our faces before doing our best to hide them. She handed me the receipt. "Thank you for stopping in, Reid. Come again anytime."

"Always, Fox." I took a sip of the now cooled latte. Fucking perfect. Of course it was, Charlotte made it. "I'll be here every day."

Her laugh probably meant she thought I was joking, but I was dead serious.

9

Charlotte

The morning after my ex showed up in Rosewood, I requested an extra session with my therapist. I was thankful Reid was there after it happened. Setting up the store with him was enough to distract me from the worst of the panic, but that night I couldn't stop thinking about whether or not Alex would come back.

So I had an impromptu therapy session. On the drive out I congratulated myself for dealing with the situation in such a responsible way. This asshole would not control my life. I was determined to continue on this great path I started paving after moving to Rosewood.

My therapist said he was impressed I showed too. The approval of men never meant much to me, but I did feel a little satisfaction at gaining the favor of the old man. As I explained what happened and we went over my feelings about it, he then decided to challenge me.

Since I proved that I could rely on others by reaching out to my therapist, he wanted me to also try relying on my friends.

I already opened up to Reid a little last night. Which left me with Dylan.

I called Dyl on my way out of the therapist's office. "Hey, so when you said you would be willing to hang out today were you joking or serious?"

"I told you anytime, Char. Did something happen?"

"Yeah, but I can tell you when I get there. You don't start work today, do you?"

"Nope, my first day is tomorrow."

"How about I bring over some sushi and smoothies?"

"Charlotte Fox, you know me so well," she said dreamily.

Walking up the steps of Dylan's apartment building with a strawberry banana smoothie and a platter of various sushi rolls in hand, I hurried to the door. Missing my best friend was hard. The double doors in front of me opened to reveal a smiling Dyl.

"You're here!" She threw her arms around my neck and I did my best not to drop our food. She took a step back to get a good look at me. "You look happy, too. Let me hold this for you." Her hands claimed the smoothie for herself.

"I stopped at the Hibachi place that you like and convinced them to make me an entire platter." I held up the tray to show off the goods. Dylan held the door open for me and gave me a well deserved grin.

We made our way upstairs and settled onto the couch. Chopsticks in hand, Dylan turned to me and twirled the utensils in the air. "Well, start talking!"

I moved a few rolls that I wanted to try to my plate while considering where to start. "So getting everything set up for the bookstore has been great. And I've got my food truck ordered for the cafe, so I will have plenty of stock when we open."

Dylan nodded. She was clearly waiting for me to drop the bomb as to why I was in such a rush to see her today. "Alex showed up in Rosewood yesterday. He came to the shop."

Her eyes widened and I thought they might pop out of her head like a cartoon. "He showed up in Rosewood?"

"Yep." I tried a piece that had crab and spicy mayonnaise. "These are good."

I looked up to see Dylan still processing. "He showed up asking about the ring. Apparently he felt entitled to it and asked me to return it. I told him to fuck off and he got all in my face until my neighbor showed up," I explained.

"Your neighbor?" she asked.

Of course that was the piece of information she would pick up on. "Yeah, the guy that runs the diner next door."

"Is he hot?"

My eyes rolled. Reid is hot, but I would never admit it. "He's my neighbor. We went to high school and played volleyball together. Well sort of, I was obviously on the girls team, but we practiced together a lot. And played practice matches against each other."

"*What?*" Dylan was leaning forward with her body fully turned toward me.

"Yeah, why is that shocking?"

She fixed her posture by straightening her back. "You have a high school sweetheart and you didn't tell me?"

Now I was the one leaning forward. "Where the hell did you get high school sweetheart out of that?"

"Oh come on, you have literally never mentioned a man to me before other than Alex. This is big. You were on the same sports team, and I bet you even did that weird arguing-flirting thing you love doing with men."

My eyebrows scrunched together. "Arguing-flirting thing?"

She laughed into her smoothie. "Yeah, you practically get a hard on when you argue. It's like the only time I ever see you flirt."

I packed that weird tidbit into the back of my brain to never think about again. "Reid and I are friends. We weren't even really friends back in high school, we only really ever talked about volleyball since we played the same position."

"But you're friends now?" Her obnoxious eyebrow raise made my eyes roll again, but a smile pulled at my lips.

"Yeah, he's been helping with the cafe." I paused and remembered my therapist's advice about opening up. "And he distracted me after Alex showed up, so that was nice."

"Sounds like a very *hot* distraction. I've only ever seen volleyball players in those matches you watched at the bar, but I'm pretty sure they were all hot. Lots of muscles. And tall!"

I shoved her lightly with my foot. "I'm a volleyball player too, you know? I am certainly not all muscle."

"Shut it, you're ruining my fantasy." Dylan continued drinking her smoothie until it was half gone. "So how do you feel about Alex showing up? How did he even find you?"

That was a question I had asked myself late at night when I was alone. "I have no idea. But I keep my doors locked now, so it shouldn't be a problem anymore."

Dylan shot me a worried glance. "It's just a ring. He should get over it."

I nodded. "Right, hopefully."

The rest of the night was spent catching up. Dylan talked about her job and by the time night rolled around I was too exhausted to drive home. She offered to share her bed, so we got comfy and fell asleep with no complaints.

10

Nick

Last night I checked for Fox's car as usual, and found the alley behind our stores empty. There was no bright blue bubbly car in sight, so my anxiety crept in. She was a grown woman, so she probably just went out to do whatever Charlotte Fox did for fun.

Instead of getting ready for bed I decided to go to my office. My diner had officially been open for two years, and with the cafe opening next door again I decided it was a good idea to focus on marketing. A food blogger that I followed for years recently posted that they were in the state. She traveled up and down the east coast trying out restaurants like mine. It could be a great opportunity, so I reached out and offered her a free dinner.

I checked my email every hour since I sent that offer days ago. Still nothing yet, but I would be stoked to have someone critique my food. After opening the diner, my love of food had only grown, but I felt a lack of competitiveness compared to working in high class restaurants across Europe.

A rabbit hole swallowed me whole as I scoured the internet looking for critics and other bloggers that I could invite to the diner. I wanted to impress someone that was known in the food world. Preparing food for my customers brought me unmeasurable pride, but sometimes I felt like I needed to be challenged more.

Once my deep dive was finished, my muscles ached from being still for so long. Leaning back in my chair, I stretched and let out an obnoxious yawn. The time read two AM as I sat up again. I stood to go take a peek out my back door and found yet again that the back alley was empty. Where the hell was she?

I sighed and forced myself to go to bed. Fox could take care of herself better than anyone. From what little she and Evangeline told me it sounded like Fox grew up without parents around, and she had no issue moving out to the city and fending for herself after high school.

The night was long and cold, and no matter how many times I tossed and turned I could not get comfortable. Summer was in full swing, so crickets were chirping and frogs were croaking. There was one cricket in particular that sounded like it was right up against my damn window.

Waking up felt like being hit over the head with a pan. I got up anyway and prepared for a long day at the diner. Tuesdays were always exhausting because I was the head chef from lunch to dinner, and we always had a major rush after soccer practice let out. Heading downstairs, the first thing I did was check the alley. Still no car.

I was beginning to get worried. Somehow I didn't have Fox's number yet, so I couldn't even call or text to make sure she was okay. Cursing myself for not getting it sooner, I headed to the prep table to start gathering ingredients for my blueberry muffins.

Muffins were made, baked, and cooled by the time my sous chef walked in the door. "Hey, Jace."

"Hey, man." Jace put away his wallet and phone in the back and went to grab an apron. "You see that order I put on the back board?"

My hands stopped chopping onions. "What order?"

Jace walked back in the room. "For twelve o'clock today. Twenty burgers and fries to-go. They called during dinner rush last night and I realized I forgot to remind you before I left."

I finished chopping the onion. "Yeah, it shouldn't be a problem. Come finish this for me, will you?"

Jace took over my position at the chopping board and I washed my hands before heading to the front door. Jace called, "Where are you going?"

"Be right back, just going to check next door."

The sun was just starting to rise as I looked down the street. Her car wasn't out front either, so I rechecked the back alley again. When I found it as I left it I walked up to the back door and knocked until my hand was sore. Nothing.

Using the key I had, when she didn't invite me over, felt wrong. I sighed and paced back and forth in the alley until a car pulling up caught my eye. Fox parked in her usual spot and I walked to her car, ready to perform my interrogation.

"Are you okay? Where the hell were you?" I paused at her confused face. This was really none of my business. Charlotte wasn't technically mine, and we were nothing more than friends.

Her eyebrow quirked at me. "I'm sorry, do I know you?"

"Nicholas Reid, I own the diner next door." She tapped her finger to her bottom lip and turned her eyes to the side as if she was genuinely trying her best to remember who I was.

"Oh! Right. You're the guy just right next door." I stared and waited for her to finish her dramatics. "Nicholas Reid." She smirked and looked me up and down.

"Well, are you going to let me out of my car?" Her playful smile only grew as I took a step back and opened the car door for her. I looked down to see her wearing the same jeans and oversized band tee as she was wearing yesterday. My head pounded as I tried putting together the possible explanations.

Out of the corner of my eye, I noticed a couple of lights glowing on her dashboard. "What the hell is that?"

"A maintenance light. One of my tire pressure sensors is broken, and it's expensive to fix, so I just look to make sure they're not low." She shrugged at me.

Then she got out of the car and stood up to face me. "I was worried something happened with your ex. Your car wasn't here last night when I went to bed." That stole the smile from her face, and I cursed myself for being the cause.

"Oh, no I still haven't heard anything from him. I was at Dylan's." My fist clenched. Who the *fuck* was Dylan? Friends. Fox and I were only friends and I needed to stay grounded in that or else I would come off as a complete lunatic.

I needed to get back to the diner. "Okay, I'm glad you're safe. It might be helpful to have your number in case we ever need to contact each other."

Her playful smile returned in full. "First you look for my car, and now you're asking for my number? Reid, be careful or I might just think you have feelings for me."

If only she knew. "Yeah, it's not even six in the morning, Fox.

Can we cool it with the teasing until after the sun is up?" I tried to keep my face from heating up while I motioned for her phone.

We exchanged numbers and I walked her to her back door. "I hope you had fun with your friend." Oh, I just could not help myself could I?

"I did, thanks. Dyl is planning a trip here soon, so maybe you two could meet then." Right, because I was so excited to meet *Dyl*.

"Right, I have to get back to the diner. Bye, Fox."

She waved to me and I stalked off to forcefully beat eggs while Jace gave me a concerned side eye. Who the fuck was Dylan? Was he someone she met recently? Why the hell did she spend the night with him?

11

Charlotte

The drive home from Dylan's was nice. I hadn't enjoyed car rides by myself in a long time, since driving in the city usually only lasted for a few minutes. Which meant it wasn't worth even putting on music. Now as I drove home, I put on my favorite 90s pop songs and sang along with the windows down.

Rosewood felt like home now, and that was somehow a relieving thought. After deciding to move in with Alex I felt a little at ease, but a small thought always lingered in the back of my mind that it could all slip away. Now there was none of that lingering anxiety to unpack.

Reid ran up to my car and questioned me on where I was last night. I felt a little guilty that he was worried about my well being. I didn't think about him connecting it to Alex coming to town, but it was endearing that he looked out for me.

I made my way inside and set down my bags with sigh. A laundry list of to-do's was waiting for me upstairs to prepare for the cafe re-opening, but I really needed to take a shower first. Being clean and warm from the hot water sounded nice.

Grabbing my bags again and heading upstairs to change out of my clothes, I paused when I heard a scratching noise. It stopped a second later, so I continued on with closing the door to my loft and stripping before jumping in the shower.

I dried off with a clean towel and grabbed my lotion to start moisturizing. My daily walks had returned the color to my skin, and I tried to remember the last time my skin was this shade. The circles under my eyes that I thought were due to getting older had improved too. I inspected my face in the mirror to look for any other differences since moving out of the city.

My hair was silkier, which could be due to the nutritional meals Reid kept giving me. They were always delicious, but he made sure they were balanced too. He started making me give scores to every dish I tried. Every single one was a ten in my eyes, but I played along and gave him a random number each time based on something totally unrelated to the taste.

After getting dressed in comfy joggers and a tank top, I went to check out my fridge in hopes of finding some breakfast. An empty fridge stared back at me. I could just head over to Reid's, but the idea of letting him wonder who Dylan was sounded much more fun.

A sound at my back door pulled me out of my contemplation. As I got closer it was clear someone was pounding on my door so I started talking, "Reid, what's your excuse-"

There was a dog sitting in front of me. A big dog, with floppy ears and puppy dog eyes sitting at my back door and staring at me. For a moment I stood frozen, turning my head to look both ways in the alley in search of any witnesses.

Then the dog burst through the door past my legs and ran

into the store. A squeak fell past my lips before I started following him. "Hey, dude. Hold on! This is not your home."

He clearly wasn't interested in a conversation, because he just continued running around through the store, sniffing every inch of the place. Finally, he stopped near the front door and sat, staring at me.

"Who do you belong to, buddy?" The scruff of his neck did not hold a collar. So either he had escaped it, which seemed totally plausible considering this situation, or he was a stray.

All I got in response was a yawn. What the hell do I do with a dog? Calling animal control sounded extreme, and despite his pushiness, he seemed sweet. I picked up my phone to call the only person who I believed could get themselves into a situation like this.

"Hey, Char-"

"A dog broke into my store, what do I do with it?"

"Well I would say it's best to call the authorities so they can take it to pup-jail. Breaking and entering is a serious offense, it could be a hardened criminal."

I sighed. "Seriously, Dyl. What do I do in this situation? It doesn't have a collar and I know nothing about dogs."

She laughed at my stress. "Take it to the vet. And stop calling it an 'it'."

"But how do I take it to the vet? It's not like I have a leash and collar hanging around."

"I don't know, use your creativity to lure it there. You'll do just fine, Steve Irwin."

She hung up with a click, and I remembered that today was her first day of work. I should have congratulated her or given her some advice, but I had a dog criminal to deal with first.

I bent down and stuck my hand out for him to sniff. After

checking to make sure he was actually a 'him' I stood back up and walked behind the counter to find something he could drink out of. He seemed pleased with the paper cup filled with water that I offered him.

He drank and managed to spray water all over the cafe in the process. Then we headed upstairs to find something tasty, so I could get him to follow me to my car. My empty fridge once again greeted me. I grabbed a half-empty package of cheese slices and turned to him.

"Do you like cheese?" I threw a piece on the ground and he sniffed before eating it.

"Okay, then. We're in business."

We headed back downstairs and I slipped on my shoes before grabbing my purse. Leaning down and offering him another piece of cheese I spoke, "Okay, you're going to follow me, and I'm going to take you to people that can help you find your home. Sound good?"

He stared in response and softly retrieved the cheese I offered. I opened the door and we were in the alley walking to my car. Half expecting him to bolt off, I was surprised when my cheese tactic actually worked, he trotted next to me up to my car. He ate another piece from one hand while I opened the back door to my car with my other.

Then I threw half a piece of cheese into the back seat. "Go on, jump in." But he sat and stared at me again. "Get in the car please." I wildly gestured for him to jump in the seat, somehow the dog didn't understand my over dramatic hand movements.

Out of ideas, I decided to sit in my front seat with the back door open. A second later he hopped into the car. Well, I'll be damned, I needed to add the title of dog whisperer to my resume, and I would totally be bragging to Dylan about that later.

I got up to close the back door, and then returned to my seat. He stayed standing in the back seat with his head poking up to the front seat next to mine. While trying not to think about the brown fur that would cover my seat, I pulled up google maps to the vet in town and began driving. The feeling of his doggy breath was right up against my cheek the entire drive.

Once we arrived in the parking lot, we continued our game of cheese dash. I opened the door and the person at the front desk gave us an incredulous look. "Ma'am your dog needs a leash to be in here."

I cringed. "Sorry, I just found him on the street." More like he found me. "And I was wondering if you could help me find his owners? He doesn't have a collar."

She got up and grabbed something before returning to us. Slipping a leash around his neck, she turned to me. "That makes more sense. I'll take him back and we can scan him to see if he has a chip. If so, it should have his owner's information."

"Great, thank you." I awkwardly looked around the very white lobby. "Should I wait here?"

The woman gave me a small smile. "Sure, it shouldn't take long. I'll let you know if we find one."

I slowly moved to sit down in one of the stiff waiting chairs. The office contained strange artwork of various animals with human smiles plastered on their faces, so I spent my time staring at them until a vet walked back with my dog. *The* dog. Not mine.

"There was no chip, so unfortunately it seems he's a stray," she informed me.

Shit. "Okay, what does that mean? Does he stay here with you?"

"No, we don't have boarding unfortunately. He'll have to go to the county, or if you would like to foster him for now, you can until someone wants to adopt him." She looks down at him. "He is an adult and looks to be some kind of pit-mix, so that could take a while."

"County? He would go to the pound?" She nodded.

Double shit. His puppy dog eyes stared into my soul again. I didn't want him to go to the pound, but I also had no freaking clue what to do with a dog. "Okay, I'll take him. Can I keep this leash?"

The vet nodded. "Since he wasn't chipped we went ahead and gave him vaccinations. You'll need to pay attention for the next hour to make sure he doesn't have any kind of reaction."

Jesus Christ. "Okay, what does that mean?"

She gave me a list of things to look out for that seemed pretty noticeable. "And what sort of stuff should I buy him? I'm not a dog person, so I have no idea how this works."

Grabbing a notepad from the front desk, she started writing down what I assumed was a list of supplies for me. Thank God. A list I could do. She handed it over and smiled at me again. "Good luck. Just remember to give him food and water, that's the most important thing."

"Got it." Food and water. I could manage that.

We made our way back to my car with the thin leash that was now tied around his neck with not too much trouble. I had to pull out the cheese again to get him to jump in the car before getting in myself. Pulling up to the pet store, I made sure to tuck the list she made in my pocket and coaxed the dog to follow me into the store.

Thirty minutes and three hundred dollars later, we were back in my car and headed home. I rolled the window down for him, but he continued to put his head right next to mine. "So, you're going to need a name."

He sniffed my cheek. Pets weren't my thing, my mother couldn't take care of me growing up, much less me plus another being that wasn't necessary. Ever since then, I had pretty much just been fending for myself, so pets weren't even on my radar.

"How about Link? Do you like that name?" Dylan introduced the Legend of Zelda games to me back when we were roommates. This dog definitely seemed to like adventure, so the name fit him.

This time he licked my cheek. "Link, it is."

Carrying a dog bed, bag of food, and basket filled with about a million other things into the store, I dropped the leash as soon as the back door closed behind us. We walked out into the main floor of the cafe where I set down everything I was holding onto the middle of the floor.

"Okay, Link. Here is your stuff." I laid out his bed flat and grabbed the bag of food and bowls I bought. Returning with a bowl of food and one of water I set them down near the counter. "This is where you can eat and drink."

He sat staring at me until I undid the leash around his neck. "How about we put on your new collar? It's a bright blue one like Scooby Doo." I situated the collar around his neck and he walked over to sniff at the food when I was done.

I sat at one of the cafe tables while I watched him eat. When he was done he walked back over and sat in front of me to stare at me again. "Okay, done with that? Look here." I grabbed his basket and pulled out one of the ten toys I bought. "Here you go. This is for you to play with."

Link watched me set the stuffed pig gingerly at his feet. "Do your thing. Play with it."

He looked down at the pig and then back at me with a bored expression. "Not a fan of toys, got it. Well I have work to do, so I'll leave you to your own devices."

I started to go upstairs to grab my laptop with the list of what else I needed to do for the store. Link followed right after me like a shadow. Why the hell was he following me? The equivalent of doggie Disneyland was right behind us.

We went upstairs and returned to the cafe with my laptop. He laid down on the cold hardwood near me even though there was a perfectly comfy bed a couple of feet away. I huffed and ignored the strange behavior, continuing my to do list was the top priority today.

Link watched as I set up social media, ordered t-shirts, and designed custom bookmarks for the store. The goal was to have Brewing Pages plastered across as many surfaces as possible. Hours passed and Link stayed in his same spot on the hard floor. I was beginning to think something was wrong with him, what if he was sick and this was a symptom of his vaccinations? Reid should have been the one caring for this dog, I had no clue what I was doing.

I called the vet and they assured me that laying on the floor for hours was perfectly normal dog behavior. The dog and I held eye contact as I hung up the phone. "Am I doing something wrong? Are you happy here or do you need something?"

He huffed and got up to walk over to me. At least he could walk. I offered a hand to pet him and he leaned into it. His entire body weight started to lean against me as I rubbed the side of his stomach. I let out a chuckle at his obvious content.

We stayed that way for a few minutes before I broke our trance. "I've gotta get back to work, bud. Why don't you lay on the bed this time?"

I walked to the back of the store to grab a box and returned to find him staring at a bird outside. Setting the box on the table, I started untangling string light decorations I was planning on hanging up. After grabbing a ladder, I carefully used the exposed pipes on the ceiling to hang up the lights. Hopefully, if I did it right, these lights would provide some pretty mood lighting to the cafe.

Dusting off my hands, I looked up to see my hours of hard work. The lights looked beautiful, especially because now it was beginning to get dark outside. I turned to Link, who had been pleasant company throughout the day. "How about a walk before bed?"

His ears perked up, and I wondered if he really had never had an owner before. We got ready and took a nice long stroll in the cool evening air. Walking around downtown Rosewood had become one of my favorite things to do here, and it was even nicer to have a friend to show it to. Even if he did walk on four legs.

"Careful of the bike, Link. I call this guy Lightning McQueen because he always goes way too fast and wears bright red pants everyday."

Toward the end of our walk, Link used the bathroom finally and I had the pleasure of figuring out how poop bags work. He seemed very pleased with himself though, because he happily pranced all the way back home. I got ready for bed after and left my bathroom to find Link laying on the floor next to my bed.

"You aren't going to sleep downstairs are you?" I smiled at his stare and went to grab his dog bed to put near him. At least it was there if he changed his mind. Sleeping with a huge animal nearby was not an experience I had ever had before. But I eventually fell asleep to the sound of his snores.

Until a burst of noise woke me up.

12

Charlotte

My sleep-fogged brain was slow to function. There was noise, loud noise, and it sounded like water, but it wasn't supposed to rain tonight. I shot out of bed and stood up. Link started barking as I slipped on some flip flops and made my way to the stairs.

I turned to the dog. "You have to stay here, okay?"

Shutting the door slowly, I turned to run downstairs as the noise grew louder. I turned and ran through to the main floor of the cafe to see what was causing it. "Shit!"

Water was pouring down on bookshelves from the pipe in the ceiling. Pages were soaked through and water pooled onto the floor as I slipped through it to get to the books. At first I tried to move the entire bookshelf, but quickly realized it was way too heavy.

Then I began grabbing armfuls of books and throwing them to the side of the store that wasn't pouring down with water. I was in full panic mode by the time I heard Reid pounding on my back door. Muttering a string of curses to all of my past ancestors, I made my way in my flip flops to let him in.

He looked at me drenched in water and ran past to see the two sprinklers that were flooding my cafe and the bookshelves that sat right beneath them. "Shit. I'll go turn off the water."

Reid ran back out of the door and I had no damn clue where he was going. I continued throwing books out of the stream of water until I heard a loud screech and the water slowed to a stop. He ran back in a few minutes later with a huge squeegee in hand.

"You okay?" He asked. I nodded.

A laugh spilled from my lips while I looked around. At least a quarter of my books were unsalvageable and another quarter were possibly damaged too. I started going to the books that had only been sprayed a bit to lay them out and dry.

"How the hell is this possible? There isn't a fire, and only a couple of the sprinklers turned on." I threw a soaked book to the ground. "What the fuck did I do to deserve this?"

"Nothing, Fox." Reid looked up at the ceiling before staring at me for a moment. "You hung up lights?"

"Yes, but I suppose those are ruined too now." I continued looking for salvageable books with my back turned to him.

Reid sighed. His pause made me turn to look at him. "What?"

"You can't hang things from the sprinkler system," he murmured.

"What?"

"The red poles you hung your lights from? You can't hang things on them. It can tamper with the sprinkler head, so they can burst out of nowhere." He looked to the ground. "Luckily it was only two of them."

I blinked at his guilty expression. "This is my fault."

"You didn't do it on purpose, Fox. It's not a big deal. Books can dry out, right? It's just water."

"I can't sell these." I picked up another book that was dripping wet with fear saturating my voice. "They are completely ruined."

Reid stopped squeegee-ing to gently take the book from my hand. "We'll figure it out. It's okay."

My head shook rapidly as I looked down at the floor that was covered in water. "What was I thinking? I can't do this."

"You can." His hand gently held my elbow until I looked at him. "You can do this. I'm here to help when you need me."

I let out a slow breath and closed my eyes. "I decided to open a bookstore on a whim and then flooded the damn place." A pitiful laugh escaped me again. "If that's not a sign, then I don't know what is."

"It's three in the morning and you've just woken up to your store flooding. Now isn't the time to make any major decisions." His voice was comforting and I almost fell asleep standing up listening to it. "We're going to clean this up and then you'll go back to bed for a good night's rest. We can talk about it more in the morning."

I nodded and looked around. "What do I do?"

Reid walked around the counter to find my stack of empty boxes. "I'll clean up the floor. You start with the books you think you can save and set them out. Then we can put the unsavable ones in boxes. Okay?"

"Okay." We worked in silence. Nick finished cleaning up the floor pretty quickly and wiped down the bookshelves with towels while I emptied them. Together we set out books that only got a little water face up to dry out overnight.

He turned to me. "You did good. These books should be just fine after a few hours, right?" I nodded again. "We've done everything we can do tonight. I'll take these boxes to the dump in the morning. Why don't you go to bed?"

I looked up at his handsome face. It was clear he was sleeping before he came here because his hair was a wreck and his shirt was inside out. The sweatpants he wore looked comfortable and I suddenly had the urge to invite him into my bed and lay in those arms that were stretching out the sleeves of his shirt.

"Thank you, Reid." His eyes widened. He pulled me into his arms and I let my head rest against his chest.

"Anytime, Fox. Will you be okay on your own tonight?" I nodded. He slowly pulled back to see my face. "Seriously, there will be no skipping town. You're just going to bed and we can talk about it in the morning."

"Mhm. In the morning," I mumbled. His intense eyes didn't leave mine as he backed away and started walking to the door.

"Goodnight. Sweet dreams, you come get me if anything else happens. At all."

"I will. Goodnight."

I locked the door behind him and headed back upstairs to Link. He whined when he saw me and licked at the water covering my arms and legs. Mindlessly, I dried myself off and picked out dry clothes before rolling back in bed and inviting Link into it to cuddle with me.

13

Nick

Charlotte showed up in my diner earlier than I expected the next morning. I planned on checking on her a little later, since I expected she would want to sleep in after the events last night. But I was glad to know she still wanted to see me too.

She walked up to the counter and sat down on a stool with a tired smile on her face directed at me. "Hey, Reid."

"Fox. You woke up early. What can I get for you?" I said with my own smile matching hers. Relief flooded my body at the sight of her smile.

"I woke up to your friend from the fire department checking out my sprinklers. You really didn't need to do that." She sighed and rolled her eyes at me. "I need grilled chicken and a blueberry muffin to-go please."

My eyebrow raised at her order. "His name is Clay, and yes I did. Grilled chicken?"

"And a blueberry muffin," she corrected. Charlotte Fox was up to no good.

"Are you ready to talk about the store? I can come over to help with those books-"

"That's okay. I want to do it myself since I'm the moron that caused the mess," she said.

"I really don't mind Fox-"

"You've done more than enough, Reid. Thanks for throwing out those damaged books for me."

With that pitiful smile, she could ask me to rip my heart out and serve it on a plate for her and I would do it. "You're welcome."

I called out the grilled chicken order to Jace and walked back over to Fox. The bell chimed at the door and I looked up to see Ash, Georgia, and Ruth. I walked around the counter to catch Ruthie.

"We're getting a fish today!" She exclaimed as I spun her around in my arms.

I set her back down and shot my brother a look. "A fish?"

Georgia laughed and moved to go sit at the counter next to Charlotte. "Yeah, we thought it would be a good first pet for Ruth. Ash said no to a dog." She said with a pouty face in his direction.

"We have no need for a dog. Your cat is more than enough chaos in the pet department." Ash helped Ruth up to sit on a barstool and sat himself down next to her. He looked over to see Charlotte down the row of stools. "Oh, hey Charlotte."

She smiled back at him. "Hey, Ashton. I'm on your side. A dog is way too much effort."

Georgia looked confused back and forth between Charlotte and me. I intercepted the conversation, "Georgia, this is Charlotte, my girlfriend." I pointed between the two. "Fox, this is Georgia. She moved to Rosewood about a year ago."

Pause. Where the fuck did that come from? Charlotte looked just as frozen as I felt at my words. I got so used to referring to her as mine in my head I somehow let the words actually come out of my mouth. A few seconds and our faces switched back to normal.

Charlotte confidently turned to Georgia and smiled. "Hey, nice to meet you. Why did you decide on Rosewood?" She recovered faster than I did from my girlfriend slip-up, but it was out there now.

"I honestly looked at a map of the state and thought the name was cute. I always wanted to move somewhere I'd never been before. After I started researching, it seemed like the perfect small town, just what I was looking for," Georgia said politely.

Fox's eyebrows raised. I guessed she was thinking that she couldn't imagine ever choosing to live in Rosewood of all places. "Nice, it seems to have been the right decision." Her head tilted from Ash back to Georgia.

Ashton wrapped an arm around Georgia and smiled at her blush. "It sure was, peach." And he leaned over to kiss her on the cheek.

I caught Charlotte observing the couple, but she pulled her gaze away quickly. Ashton focused back on Fox again. "So, how's the new store coming along? I heard it's going well."

Georgia gasped. "Oh, you're the owner of the new bookstore and cafe!"

"Yeah, I am." Char laughed at Georgia's excitement.

"I am so excited for it. I've always told Ash, the one thing missing in Rosewood is a bookstore."

Char took a sip of the water I set in front of her and I noticed her subtle wince. "You should definitely stop by sometime. I'll give you a pre-opening tour, we've got all kinds of books."

I tuned out as the two women started talking about books and Georgia's writing career. Ashton waved me over to his side of the bar. He ordered breakfast for the three of them and then started giving me his annoying ass smile that meant he thought he knew something he shouldn't.

"Glad to see you happy, brother." Ashton smirked.

My eyes rolled. "You too, brother." His smile widened as he took my words to mean he was correct in his assumption.

Fox stuck around and made small talk while they ate their breakfast. Georgia, Ashton, and Ruth left soon after wolfing down their plates at record speed. Charlotte turned to Georgia as they were getting up to go, "Seriously, stop by sometime. I'll hook you up with a discount and everything."

Georgia happily agreed, and once again I was left alone with Charlotte at my bar. She turned her body until it was fully facing me. "Did I hit my head at some point?"

Her eyes on me made my head spin, maybe I was the one that hit my head at some point. Her full lips turned up at the corners in one of my favorite smiles of hers.

"Not to my knowledge."

"Did we wake up in an alternate dimension? Or did the timelines get crossed somewhere?"

"This isn't a sci-fi movie, so no."

She tapped on the counter as she continued to think up more ridiculous questions of hers. I interrupted before we got stuck in this circle for another thirty minutes. "Ash has been bugging me about settling down. And I figured it solved your problem the other day, so it would be best to just keep pretending for a while."

Her eyebrows scrunched. "And you didn't think to consult me on this?"

"Should I have asked if you could step aside for a quick conversation before introducing you to Georgia? It was more of a spur of the moment thing."

"Well it sounds like you've been picturing this for a while, Reid."

She had no fucking clue. "Only in my dreams."

Now she was beaming at me. "You're flirting with me."

I scoffed and started wiping down the counter. Her eyes followed me as I worked and I hoped to God the heat I felt in my face wasn't actually visible to anyone else. My server walked up and let me know he was taking his break.

Once the heat subsided I looked up at her to see her eyes practically twinkling with amusement. My ears must be fucking red at this point. The bell rang with another customer and I went to help them. Ten minutes came and passed as I served customers and she sat there watching me.

My server returned from break and I watched from afar as Fox slipped him her card and he rang her up at the register. There was no way she was paying in my damn diner. She must have known I'd say that or else she wouldn't have asked him to ring her up.

I returned as he slid her the card and receipt. Her keys remained on the counter behind her glass of water, but I didn't remind her to grab them. She gathered up her to-go box and waved with her free hand. "Thanks for the food, I'll see you around Reid."

My eyes narrowed at her. "You're welcome. I'm coming over later to talk about the book situation, okay?"

Fox just rolled her eyes. "I can handle it. But okay, I'll see you then, Reid."

The vulnerable Charlotte Fox from last night was long gone,

and I couldn't help but wonder if this was an act or if she truly did have it handled. I waved back to her and shoved her keys into my pocket before helping Jace in the kitchen.

During my lunch break, I did my usual routine of checking my email to see if anyone had gotten back to me about visiting the diner. I was pushed back in my chair, but sat up quickly and moved my plate out of the way when I saw Lane Gilbert had gotten back to me. Holy shit.

My eyes skimmed her email until I read the words 'See you soon'. She planned on visiting my diner and writing a review for her blog in a few weeks. This was big, finally someone knowledgeable in fine dining would be trying my restaurant and potentially bringing in customers from all across the state to Rosewood.

Lane Gilbert had a cult following, and her fans were willing to travel far and wide to try food she raved about. I was stoked to have the opportunity to impress her and the people that read the food blog. Charlotte had been rating my food lately, and it gave me a sense of confidence in my talent that I hadn't had in a long time.

After replying to the email letting Lane know that I was looking forward to meeting her, I went to tell Jace I would be out for a bit. It was hot as hell outside today. I flipped my hat to sit backwards and pulled out my phone to call a friend.

14

Charlotte

Grilled chicken in tow, I headed back to my apartment to eat breakfast with Link. He cuddled with me all night long, and I felt like I owed him for being such a good boy, so I put his grilled chicken in one of his bowls to eat next to me on the floor. We sat by a cafe table while I ate my muffin.

I stared at the now empty bookshelves while I ate. Thousands of dollars of inventory was now gone because I wanted to hang up pretty lights, how pathetic. After eating my muffin, I got up and began moving the dry books back to their shelves. Link once again seemed to enjoy watching me work as I pulled out my laptop and began ordering the books that I lost.

The urge to pull out my phone and call Dylan to buy plane tickets to wherever was the soonest available was strong. But I had poured my blood, sweat, and tears into this cafe over the last month. Literally. The people of Rosewood were counting on me too, I promised a damn bookstore cafe, so the people were going to get a bookstore cafe. Even if it killed me.

A knock on the door grabbed my attention. Standing in front of it was someone I had seen just that morning and another that I hadn't seen in over ten years. I walked over to the door to open it with a smile on my face.

"Reese, it's been a while." My old teammate threw herself at me with a hug and squeezed me tight. Reese Finch was the human equivalent of a care bear.

She pulled away with a huge smile lighting up her freckle covered cheeks. Her curly hair was longer than when I'd last seen it and her overall dress hugged her curves perfectly. "How is it that everyone I know has told me that you've been in town and I'm only just now seeing you?"

"I've been holed up in this place working." I jabbed my thumb behind me. Turning to Georgia, I smiled again and we went in for a quick hug. "Long time no see."

She laughed quietly. "Yeah, it's been forever."

Reese grabbed my hand. "So, I know you're working on this super important cafe reveal, which I want to hear all about by the way. But, we were wondering if you wanted to have a girl's day with us. Georgia told me she met you this morning and I thought you should join."

I looked back and forth between the two women. Their faces lit up into devious smiles now, whatever it was they were smiling about I totally wanted in. "Alright, I'm game. Just let me grab my bag."

Shutting the door so Link didn't escape, I went to fetch my bag. Then I turned to Link, "Will you be okay on your own? You can look after the shop right?" He yawned at me.

"Just in case," I murmured. I grabbed a third bowl and gave him an extra bowl of water. He stared at me as I set it down and I felt just as silly as the way he was looking at me. Then I grabbed his stuffed pig toy and set it on his bed next to him. "Be good, okay?"

He sniffed at the pig and I took that as my cue. "I'll be back soon!" I called. My hand absentmindedly looked for my keys. When I didn't find them I paused, maybe I left them in my car?

Seconds later I was standing dumbstruck in the back alley. My car was gone. As in, totally disappeared out of thin air, along with my keys. I couldn't even remember the last time I had them.

A stolen car was the last thing I could handle mentally right now. So, I sighed, turned around, and met Georgia and Reese out front without a word. "Ready to go?"

I nodded, ready to get out of my head and focus on anything else for the day. "Ready."

Parking the car in front of the last place I expected these two to go for a 'girls day', Georgia turned around in the car to look at me in the back seat. "We're getting tattoos."

Reese's grin was blinding. "You don't have to get one, but we are. We need someone to hold our hands because this is our first."

My laugh filled the car and Georgia and Reese joined in. "Okay, tattoos it is."

I flipped through a book of small tattoo designs while Reese was situated on the bed next to me. Her tattoo artist was getting his set up ready and she pulled down her shorts a little to show the area of her hip that she wanted the tattoo placed on.

"So, why a lily?" I asked absentmindedly while flipping through pages.

"I've always loved them. And it's sort of for my mom too." Meeting her gaze, I waited for further explanation. "She's not dead or anything, she just means a lot to me."

I nodded and went back to the book. Georgia walked over and sat next to me while we watched Reese get her tattoo done. "You know, I was fully expecting to go to brunch or something."

Georgia laughed. "That is much more our speed, usually. Today just seemed like a day to be adventurous."

"What are you getting?"

"A peach." She pointed to her hip too, where Reese was getting hers. I remembered that was what Ashton called her this morning and a smile pulled at my lips. "Is it crazy?"

I laughed. "Not at all. I think it's cute, it's fun too."

Georgia nodded to herself and we continued cheering on Reese and distracting her while her lily was being done. Next up was Georgia, and her peach was finished pretty quickly since it was so small. The tattoo artist started cleaning up his station.

I walked over to him and slid him a sample of the font that I liked. "Can you do this? I just want three numbers, pretty small on my hip."

Reese squeaked. "You're getting one too?"

"Yeah, I think so. We're being spontaneous right? C'est la vie."

The artist agreed and asked a few more questions before going to sketch it out and returning a few minutes later. "This look good?"

I nodded. The numbers '234' written in a standard black font were on the paper he showed me. After I was situated on the chair and pulled down my jeans to show my waist, he peeled off the back and carefully placed the stencil on my hip.

The pain wasn't as bad as I expected, but it was more annoying than anything. Thankfully, since the tattoo was small it was over quickly. Reese held my hand the entire time and she and Georgia chatted to me until it was over.

"Can we know what the numbers mean?" Reese asked.

"Yeah, it's the street address for the shop. My own version of an initiation ritual, hopefully it will bring good luck." Because I sure as hell needed it. The time I played whack a mole with thirteen mirrors clearly wasn't doing me any favors.

Care instructions were read to all three of us, and my tattoo was covered with a protective seal. We were standing up and getting ready to leave when Reid and Ashton walked through the door. Ashton made a beeline for Georgia with a curious look on his face.

"What exactly are you doing in a tattoo shop?" Then he turned to Reese. His head slowly turned to me and then back to Georgia again. "Who the hell out of you three would get a tattoo? Charlotte?"

I held up my hands in defense and smiled at Reid. "Maybe. How did you guys know we were here?"

His eyebrows shot up as he looked me up and down in search of any ink. "Where is it?"

Reese stepped in. "Actually, we all got tattoos."

The incredulous looks on Reid and Ashton's faces made us all laugh. Silence filled the group as our smiles grew and they inspected us for any signs of ink. Reid spoke first, "You're fucking with us."

"Nope. I am a first hand witness to their first tattoos, it was Reese's idea by the way. Which I think is definitely the biggest shock of all." I lifted the hem of my tank top to show a peek of the wrap that covered my hip.

Reid's eyes widened impossibly bigger. "What did you get?"

"I'll tell you later."

Ashton's hands went to Georgia's hips and she lifted the hem of her shirt too. She peeled back the protective cover to show the small peach. Ashton scrubbed a hand over his face. "Holy shit. When I saw your phone show you were at a *tattoo* shop, I thought you'd surely gotten kidnapped or something."

Georgia laughed and pushed Ashton away, so she could stick it back on. "Let's go, I'm starving." His face was incredulous as he followed her out of the tattoo shop like a puppy dog.

We all started walking toward Reese's car and Reid waved everyone else off. "We're going to walk home. See you guys later."

I turned to shoot him a look. "We are?" He nodded and set a hand on my lower back to guide me back to the sidewalk.

"Bye! Thanks for the tattoo trip. Let me know when you guys have your next girls day!" I called as Reid ushered me down the street.

Reese called back. "We will! Don't forget to rewrap it."

Reid turned to me and quietly asked. "You got a tattoo?"

I nodded and smiled. "It seemed like a good idea. I was being spontaneous and it was fun."

"I guess it's better than running," he muttered. "Is this some kind of new coping mechanism? Can we talk about what happened last night now?"

A slow breath escaped my lips. "Sure, if you want."

"First, I want to know what your tattoo is."

"It's 234, I wanted it to be somewhat meaningful and-"

"That's the number of your store. 234 Main Street." I nodded. "So that means you're staying?"

"Even with floods, car theft, and stalkers I'm staying. This is the path I've chosen and I'm going to make it work." Or at least that was my therapist's advice, working through things, and he hadn't led me astray so far.

"Car theft," he repeated.

"Oh yeah, my car is gone. Disappeared from the alley sometime this morning, and I can't find my keys so-" Reid reached into his pocket and held up my keyring. "You have my keys."

He nodded slowly with guilt written all over his face. "I should have told you. But in my defense you almost never leave during the day, so I didn't think you would notice."

My mouth gaping, I lightly shoved his shoulder. "You stole my car."

"Stealing is a bit harsh. More like improving. I took it to a shop so they could fix it for you."

My mind came up with nothing as a response. I literally could not compute what he was saying. Why would he do that? Torn between complete confusion, frustration, and happiness I laughed.

"You fixed my car."

He nodded and pulled his hat down to cover his face. "I should have told you."

"It would have been nice to know, but the good intention was there." He kicked a rock as we walked. "Thank you."

He tilted his head to look at me. "You're welcome and I'm sorry. Next time I go carjacking I'll try to tell you first."

Laughter filled my voice as I spoke, "I appreciate that, Reid. Just let me know how much you paid for it and I'll pay you back."

He scoffed. "So about the books. What do we need to do to replace them? Opening is in a few weeks, right? Will that leave enough time for shipping?"

"I'm paying for the car, Reid."

"You paid at the diner. We're even." His words held finality to them.

"You are insane, I hope you know that." All I got in response was silence. "Yeah, I should be okay to get the books back in time. I already put back the ones that we dried last night, they look great. No water damage whatsoever."

"Good, do you need money? I have savings-" I turned my shoulders to face him while we continued walking.

My hand rested on his arm while I spoke. "Reid, I have money. I'll be okay, seriously don't worry about it." Investing the rest of my savings into my business probably wasn't smart, but I was committed at this point. It was literally engraved in my body in ink.

He nodded. "But if that changes I can help."

"Got it, Reid. Now stop worrying." He chuckled at my command.

"You get one tattoo and now you think you're all that. Easy, Fox. I'm still the reigning one v one champion here." His smirk caused my footsteps to stop.

"I can kick your ass any day any time, Reid. Just say when." My eyes narrowed and he only stepped closer. I backed up to maintain eye contact without having to strain my neck, but he continued walking me backwards into the brick building behind me.

"Is that right?" He taunted. My eyes couldn't help but flit back and forth between his intense gaze and his lips. Leaning in even closer, he spoke right into my ear before backing up, "We'll have to have a rematch then."

I blinked and let out a long and slow breath. "Right, we will."

The rest of our walk home was filled with subtle glances and my head pounded while trying to figure out what was going on. Was he going to kiss me? Did I like it? I put pressure on my hip before flinching when realizing I now had a tattoo there.

He dropped me off at the store. "Take care, Fox. I'll see you later."

I nodded and waved him off. "Bye, Reid."

After closing the door, I walked past Link and up to my apartment. "What the hell was that?"

Link's wagging tail caught my attention and I turned to him. "Oh, hey buddy. Did you do a good job while I was away?" We sat together for a few minutes while I gave him pets and tried to process Reid's actions.

15

Nick

All day long I had been thinking about Charlotte Fox. At five this morning I was worrying about if she was okay after her store was flooded last night, then I spent my afternoon in a car shop helping my buddy repair her car, and after I was wondering in amazement at the fact that she got a tattoo. I could not keep up with her.

Now she walked into my diner with her relaxed confidence in joggers and a black t-shirt. She looked better than any wet dream I had ever had and I was just glad to have her in my presence. She walked up to the counter and sat down on a stool with a smile on her face directed at me. "Hey, Reid."

"Fox. What can I get for you?" I said with my own smile matching hers.

She asked for dinner and let me pick what to make for her. I loved that she trusted me with these decisions. And that she came to me to cook for her. Fox was growing fond of me.

I finished putting together her burger and walked the plate back over to the counter to put in front of her. There was plenty of work to do, so I let her eat while I rushed around the restaurant restocking and assisting where I could.

The dinner rush was dying down and Charlotte still sat there on her stool sipping on a Coke. I walked back around the counter after running out of things to do.

"Do you know how to bake?" she asked.

That was out of the blue. "I know how to. But I'm much more comfortable with cooking."

Her mischievous smile made my skin warm. "I want brownies."

"You want me to make you some?" I would do practically anything for her. She rarely asked for things, so all she needed to do was tell me how high and I would jump.

Her laugh rang throughout the diner. "I was going to make some, and maybe you could try one. Or supervise to show me if I was doing anything horribly wrong."

Was Charlotte Fox trying to invite me to hang out?

"Can you wait another hour? I can come over right when we close."

Her smile in response was all I needed. "Okay, just come over when you're ready." She hopped off of the stool and waved to my server and chef before leaving.

An hour and some change later I was opening her back door with my key and heading up the stairs. I knocked on the door to her apartment and she let me in. Her hair was up in a beautiful messy bun that I just wanted to mess up even more. Her sleepy smile felt like home.

"Hey, Fox. I brought over everything we might need." I held up the bin in my arms that had ingredients for a basic batch of brownies.

"You didn't need to do that. But I'm glad you did because I totally don't have all of this in my pantry." She looked over everything as she took it from me and set it on the counter.

We got to work mixing together all of the ingredients. Charlotte did most of the work, but I supervised and gave her pointers when necessary. This woman barely had any proper kitchen utensils, I would definitely be buying her some after this. Who doesn't own a whisk?

As she was pouring the batter into a brownie pan, some of the mixture spilled onto her finger. I watched her stare at it for a second before turning to me and smearing it across my cheek. I stood frozen before quickly shoving my own finger into the mostly empty bowl and swiping the side.

She shrieked and backed up, holding out a spatula to protect herself. She had no chance against me. I had six inches of height and a much larger wingspan than her. I leapt toward her and held her face still with my clean hand while smearing brownie batter all along the side of her face.

Charlotte gasped dramatically and used her spatula to swipe the opposite side of my face with more brownie batter. I huffed out a laugh and closed my eyes in defeat. Her laughter warmed my heart and she slid down to the floor as her body shook.

Once she caught her breath and wiped the tears from her eyes, her smile turned up to me. "Are you done yet?" I asked.

She held out a hand and I took it to help her stand on her feet. One of her fingers lifted to my cheek to steal some of the brownie batter there and she put it on her tongue. My eyes darkened and narrowed in on her mouth.

"I think I'm done now." She smirked. Returning to the sink, she washed her hands and grabbed a few paper towels to wipe at her face. I yanked them from her and wet them before cleaning up her face myself.

She focused on me intently with a smile still on her lips. Then when she was cleaned up, she grabbed paper towels of her own to clean up my mess. I did my best to lean down for her so she could reach without craning her neck.

We started a movie while waiting for the brownies to bake. I made sure to sit close to her on the couch and wrapped my arm around her shoulders. She chose not to comment on it and we snuggled in happily.

At some point her feet folded up so they were resting in my lap, and she moved her head to rest directly on my shoulder. We were fully pressed up against each other and I wanted nothing more than to let those brownies burn. Moving from that spot was no more appealing than walking into a burning building.

The oven timer rang anyway and Charlotte hopped up to go pull them from the oven. I groaned inwardly and waited impatiently for her to return.

We ate the brownies and finished up the movie in silence. I kept shooting glances her way as if she would disappear if my eyes stayed away from her for too long. When the movie finished, I sighed. That was definitely my cue to leave.

"Thanks for coming over." Charlotte sighed happily. She was happy in my presence, and that was one thing that would always cheer me up.

I nodded. "Of course, Fox. Thanks for not burning down the kitchen." Her eyes rolled, but she smiled and walked me downstairs to the backdoor anyway. After pausing for a second, I threw in an offer. "Hey, some of us are going to the beach tomorrow, if you want to join."

"The beach?" She asked and tilted her head to the side. "Well, I sort of have work to catch up on. Today I was supposed to work on designing my logo, but I got a little side tracked."

"Well, we were only going for the afternoon. Maybe you

could join after you finish," I said hopefully. "Unless you're worried you won't win our rematch."

She glared at me as I held my breath. "Okay, I'll be there."

"I'll see you tomorrow." My heart squeezed.

"Right, tomorrow." Now it was time to call up my brother and convince him to set up a beach day on short notice. I hoped to God no one was busy.

Waking up bright and early felt a little easier knowing that I would be spending the day with Fox later. I got ready and headed downstairs to get ahead of food prep for the day. Practically whistling to the 90's pop song playing over my speaker by the time Jace came in, he shot me a disgruntled look.

"It's six in the morning," he mumbled.

"Good morning to you, too." I replied.

Over the course of breakfast he asked me several times what the hell had me in such a good mood, but I just continued working until the clock hit twelve. Once it did, I left Jace in charge and headed upstairs to switch into trunks and tennis shoes.

Trotting down the stairs and heading out my back door, I knocked on Fox's door and waited not-so-patiently. It took forty three seconds for her to swing it open. Her hair was pulled back in a cute little messy bun and braid thing. She had strands falling perfectly around her face and her green eyes were bright and welcoming.

"Hey," I breathed out. She was literally breathtaking.

She chuckled and looked down to her black sneakers. "Hey, I'm ready when you are."

I nodded and we got into my car without any other words. "Do you have any music that you want to listen to?"

"Techno is actually my preferred music of choice now." Her face held not a single hint of amusement, but I knew Fox better than to let her fool me.

My eyes rolled before I reached and turned on the radio to whatever pop song was trending at the moment. "Nice try. I still can't stand it by the way, I'm traumatized from Ash's workout playlist back in high school," I grumpily muttered.

She snickered and sat back in her seat. After picking up Ash, Georgia, and Ruth, the car was filled with excited chatter and the smell of sunscreen. We all piled out of the car at the beach and grabbed chairs and a couple of coolers that were packed in my trunk.

Georgia and Fox struck up a conversation and were chatting in the sand while my brother and I got everything set up near the volleyball net. As we were finishing, Reese and Ryan walked up with a few other guys from our league team.

A practice match started up quickly, and I ran over to Fox to make sure she was okay before I jumped in. I tapped her shoulder to steal her attention away from Reese, who had a very tan Ryan Summers standing over her shoulder.

"Hey, Fox. You okay if I join in on this match? Or do you want to play?"

She looked shocked at the question, but waved me off. "Go ahead, we'll do our rematch later. I'll let you get warmed up first." Her confident grin made my heart speed up, and I could not wait to play with her again.

Hours and a few matches later, Fox had caught up with most of my friends that she hadn't seen in ten years. She was fitting in great with the group, and Ruthie seemed to take a real liking to having a group of women to hang out with.

I walked up to the three women that were sitting in beach

chairs around Ruth, who seemed to be working on a massive sandcastle. Ash was sitting on a towel next to her and acting as her personal assistant with scooping up wet sand for her buckets.

Fox looked up as I approached and I watched her eyes linger on my tan chest. She still remained covered with an oversized t-shirt over her black athletic shorts, and I was looking forward to seeing it come off. Her shoes and socks were tossed to the side and her feet were buried in the sand.

"Would you like to warm up first, so you don't have any excuses when you lose?"

Her pretty green eyes rolled. She stood up to casually take off her t-shirt and uncover a pretty blue string bikini top underneath. Now that the shirt was off I could even see the strings from her bottoms peeking out over her shorts.

Holy fuck.

The sound of her laughing brought me back to reality and I caught her waving in my face. "You alright there, Reid?"

I ran a hand over my face and did my best to focus. "Just fine, are you ready then?"

She nodded and shot me a teasing smile. "More than ready."

Our friends took a break as the two of us took up the volleyball court on opposing sides. Volleyball wasn't meant to be played without a team behind you, but Fox and I were always competitive enough to make it work somehow. She shot me another smile as she bent her knees to prepare to receive my opening serve. I caught a great view of her tits and heard her laugh as one of the worst serves I had ever done flew over the net.

Twenty minutes was all it took for us to reach match point. I was totally letting her win a few points, but I simply had an unfair advantage. Nearly every week, I was playing with my friends, and from what I was seeing, Fox hadn't picked up a volleyball since high school.

Although she *had* earned quite a few points on her own. Never in my life had I been so distracted by a bikini, it was like returning to a time in my teen years when all I could think of was tits.

I was up one, and needed only one more point to beat her. So far, I might have gone a little easy on her, but there was no chance in hell I would ever let her *win*. We went through another rally of three hits before I ultimately jumped above the net and slammed down the ball onto her side of the court.

She dove in the sand for the ball and looked up at me after watching it hit the sand. I couldn't stop myself from gloating a little as I smirked down at her. Ducking under the net, I held out my hand to help her up.

"Nice game," I offered.

Grabbing my hand, she lifted herself up. "Give me six months, and I'll beat you again. You've had about ten years of extra practice on me. All I need is six months."

A grin spread across my face and I nodded. "Six months. You can always practice with us, you know?"

"I will. Enjoy this moment while it lasts, Reid. It's all you're going to get." We stood there for a moment in the sand smiling at each other wickedly.

The rest of the day was spent being lazy and eating the sandwiches I packed for everyone. There was a frozen lemonade stand on the beach too, so I made sure to get Fox some. As the sun was setting, we all piled back in our cars to head back home.

My last stop was to drop off Fox at her door. She had a

pink tint to her cheeks where she didn't reapply sunscreen, and her hair was even messier than when I picked her up. I had never seen anything more beautiful. Every time I thought she couldn't get any prettier she always managed to prove me wrong.

We both said goodnight and she quietly went inside and locked the door behind her.

16

Charlotte

I watched as Dylan's car pulled up in front of the store and waved to her with Link's leash in my other hand. Her wide smile matched mine as her car halted to a stop and she hopped out, running toward us. The thud of her body colliding into mine in a hug made me flinch a little.

"Oh my god, you have a *dog*." I laughed and nodded. She reached out a hand to Link who politely sniffed at it before turning away. "You have a dog and you're-" her hands waved around my general direction. "Glowing. You look happy."

I chuckled that the idea of me being happy was so ground-breaking. "Yeah, I've been doing okay." Link started walking and tugged a little at the leash. "It's time for his walk, do you want to join?"

Her head nodded enthusiastically, "Of course!" Dylan had a little extra pep in her step this morning, and I was beginning to wonder why she didn't bring me a coffee since she clearly already had one.

"So, this happiness. Is that a result of the store or being in

Rosewood?" Her tone was curious, but there was a hint of amusement in there too.

I kicked a rock as we walked down the familiar brick-stoned sidewalk. "I don't know. It's a mixture, I think. The store is going well, and I guess therapy has been somewhat helpful. Rosewood isn't as bad as I remembered."

Dylan's smile brightened. "Oh yeah? Anything else?"

"No, that's all I can think of right now." I smiled at the ground. Dylan could play her games all she wanted, but that didn't mean I had to participate in them. "How is the big new job going?"

"It's great. I actually think management might be my calling, you know? All I have to do is make sure *other* people do their job. Easy as pie." I laughed at her revelation.

"Well I'm glad you finally found something for you." I sneaked a glance over at her. "We'll see how long it lasts."

She laughed and jokingly pinched my arm. "I'm not that bad!"

"How many jobs have you had in the last five years?" She scoffed and swung her arms as she walked.

"Whatever. So are you excited for opening day? It's coming up."

"I'm nervous as hell. Everything is ready on my part though, I just have to wait for the food truck to show up with everything for the cafe side of things. I've got my flyers, bookmarks, and t-shirts all set up too."

Her head turned to me. "You have flyers? We should pass them out." Dylan openly pointed at a couple walking past us on the opposite side of the street. "People are walking all around us, we could be telling them about your business!"

I pushed her hand down. "Didn't your mother ever teach

you manners?"

"No, and I much prefer it that way." She cheekily snarked. "But really, what if while you give me the official Rosewood tour today, we knock out two birds with one stone and hand out some flyers?"

I bit my lip as I contemplated her offer. It wasn't a bad idea, Dylan was great support and it was much less likely to get awkward with her by my side. "Okay, that's not a bad idea."

"So far though, this town is looking pretty damn cute. You were totally holding out on me, is that a tattoo shop over there?"

To my left was the shop I visited a few days ago with art hanging in the windows and a neon sign that was unlit. "Oh, yeah. Speaking of, I might have gotten a tattoo."

"Holy shit, no way." Dylan scanned my face with narrowed eyes to see if I was being serious. "Let me see!"

"It's on my hip, I'll show you when we get back. I don't want to pull down my leggings in the middle of the street."

Her jaw dropped as she stared at me wide eyed. "What is it?"

"It's just three numbers, 234. It's the address for the store, I wanted something commemorative. After that chaos with the sprinklers I honestly was tempted to give up, but I'm staying so I wanted it to be permanent."

Dylan's only response was to nod thoughtfully, like she was deciphering a secret code. "You really do like it here."

"I do. I really didn't think I would, but I do." We continued walking and I redirected the conversation back to Dylan's life. She gave me a very long winded update about her regular sushi place and how she was beginning to wonder if it was really a front for a drug ring.

"And the mattress store right next to it? Totally some kind

of illegal business too. I wouldn't be surprised if they were working together. Oh my god, or, what if they're rivals?"

Her usual conspiracy theories faded into the background as I watched Reid leave his shop and walk over to my door in the distance. He knocked once and then walked away after he didn't see me in the window.

"Hello? Earth to Char." A hand waved in front of my face and my ears turned back on.

I gently grabbed her wrist and put it back by her side. "I'm right here. I hear you."

Squinted eyes pointed in my direction told me she didn't believe me one bit. "What were you staring at?" She looked back toward my shop, but he was already gone.

"Nothing, just Reid was knocking on my door. I wonder if he needed me for something," I said absentmindedly.

Her smile meant no good. "Oh, well we should definitely go see what he wants. Come on, I need a very in-depth tour of this diner." Dylan latched onto my arm and she practically dragged Link and I down the street.

"I have to put Link inside. Hold on please." We returned inside the store and I took my sweet time pouring his breakfast and refilling his water bowl.

Her foot tapped impatiently on the shiny white tile. "For the love of God, Char. The bowl is clean. Fill it up and let's go. I have been dying to meet *the* Nicholas Reid."

My eyes closed as I held down a laugh because I knew she genuinely meant it. Dylan could be impatient as hell and I was definitely pushing her buttons. "Okay, Link is good to go. Let's go."

Before stepping from behind the counter I grabbed a stack of the flyers I designed for Brewing Pages and shoved them into my tote bag. Following Dylan out of the door, I made sure to lock it behind us.

The smile on Dylan's face was almost embarrassing when she saw Reid for the first time. Her cheeky grin made my face heat, but I forced myself to remain calm. We walked up to the counter and I sat in my usual stool while Dyl sat beside me.

Reid walked up to us silently and waited for me to make introductions. "Reid, this is Dylan, my friend. Dylan, Reid."

I leaned back in the stool and watched the two look at each other for the first time. Dylan's smile rivaled a kid's first time in a candy shop while Reid's face went from furrowed eyebrows to a slow revelation of some sort. He turned back to me with a smile matching Dylan's when he was done.

"This is Dylan," Reid stated with the most smug look on his face.

My head tilted as I tried to figure out what the hell he was getting at. "Yes, this is Dylan," I replied dumbly.

"I have been dying to meet you. Char has told me so much about you, and how you've been helping her out with the cafe." Dylan's blue fingernails slapped onto the counter as she emphasized how excited she was.

Reid met her smile and something in my chest burned. "*Char* has told me about you, too. I heard you two had a little sleepover at your place the other night."

Oh. Something in my brain clicked as I processed his smug attitude at seeing Dylan and his comment about the sleepover. I forgot I mentioned Dylan the other day after I had been out all night. He totally thought Dylan was a one night stand. Was that why he was worried? Was he jealous?

Those dark eyes turned back to mine and they crinkled at the corners with his smile. Reid really did have the most handsome face, and something about the dark hair paired with his eyes made him much more attractive than he was back in high school.

"Yes, and Char told me that you helped her out when that asshole showed up out of the blue. Thank you so much for that. It's not easy taking care of her from an hour away." Dylan sighed and looked down at the menu.

My eyebrows raised. Taking care of me? If anything I was the one who made sure Dylan paid her rent on time and got home after late nights at the bar.

Reid spoke up next, "I can imagine. She really is a handful, but I'm glad she had you to take care of her the day after that whole ordeal went down."

What the hell? "I am sitting right here, you know? You two can share babysitting tips later when I'm not in the room."

Dyl laughed and Reid hid his snicker by turning to the kitchen. When he collected himself, he turned back to face me. "So what can I get you two for breakfast this morning?"

* * *

"He seriously is so amazing, Char. Literally the perfect man for you. He is a dime compared to that dumbass Nickel. No- he's a nice new Benjamin." I stuck another flier to a telephone pole and hastily taped the sides.

"Uh huh." I had done my best to tune Dylan out after breakfast this morning, but she was not stopping anytime soon. The warmth I felt seeing Dylan and Reid interact made me a little nervous, but it was honestly nice having my two friends finally meet.

Now I just had to figure out why the hell I was starting to

get butterflies around Nicholas Reid. I grabbed another paper from Dylan and taped it to the next telephone pole as she strolled behind me. The breeze was perfect today, but my face still felt like it was on fire.

Dylan handed a flier to a passerby and cheerily greeted them, "Hello! My friend here is reopening the cafe on Main Street, and it's also going to be a bookstore now. It's called Brewing Pages, opening day is September 1st."

The old man waved and gave a short smile before thanking her and walking off. So far today, we made a lot of progress. Nearly the entire town had fliers on every pole, corkboard, and entryway. And Dylan was practically a citizen of Rosewood herself, she got us invited to three different dinners just today.

We finished up and decided to head back home. Despite our invitations, I had already promised Dyl we could try out Reid's Diner for dinner since she was absolutely obsessed with the man. I had half a mind to tell her to go for him herself. But I didn't.

Back at home we laid on my sofa lazily for a bit before dinner. "So, can we actually talk about it now?"

"About what?" I stared up at the ceiling while twirling my foot that was hanging over the couch arm.

"Reid. Nick. What do I call him by the way?" She sat up to get a good look at me.

"Nick, everyone else calls him Nick." I sighed.

A smile pulled at her lips. "Okay, that's a start. Do you like him?"

"Of course I like him. We're friends."

Dylan let out the most dramatic sigh ever heard. I sat up to glare at her. "We're friends, that's it. If I had to pick anyone in the world to date, it would probably be him, but I'm not sure

I'm even ready for a relationship again."

"Why is that? Are you scared after what happened with Alex?"

Scared wasn't the right word. It was closer to apathetic. If I decided to try a relationship again, and it ended up the same way my last one had, I was pretty sure I would never feel a romantic thing for another human again. That thought *was* a little scary, I supposed.

"I just don't know if it's worth the risk." Crossing my arms over the pillow, I covered my chest and pulled it close to me in a hug.

Dyl reached out and grabbed one of my hands to open my arms up again. "Even though the last one ended up being so shitty, look at where it got you. You never would have come back here and carried on your grandmother's legacy. You never would have met Nick again. Or gotten a tattoo." She squeezed my hand tightly. "That means something right?"

"I guess. I am much happier now than I was before." Was Reid worth the risk though? I wasn't even sure if he was interested in me like that. Although I definitely trusted him now, and I doubted he would ever hurt me in that way.

Her small smile made me form one of my own. Our fingers squeezed each other's hands before we let go. "And what was all of that nonsense about taking care of me? I still do your taxes, you know?"

A laugh rang around the loft apartment. "We take care of each other. You can do taxes remotely, but it would be a little weird if I forced you to go out to a bar while on FaceTime. It seems Nick has done a great job of making sure you interact with the outside world though."

Link walked over and sat beside us on the floor. Dyl's hand

reached out to pet him behind his ears, just the way he liked. I started thinking of all the ways that my friend had been looking after me without even realizing. Every time she dragged me out to a bar or concert, I thought I was doing *her* a favor. But she was right, I would have rarely left my apartment in the city without her.

My throat felt tight and I gave my best friend a wobbly smile. "Oh, therapy has made you so soft, Char. You're tearing up over how beautiful our friendship is."

We both laughed as we leaned in and hugged each other.

17

Nick

Ruth giggled as we pretended to sneak out of the diner and walk down the street with hats pulled down over our head and hoodies on over the hats. I reached for her hand and we walked at a quick pace for a six year old. When we reached the drug store on the corner, I followed her lead as she dragged me into one of the aisles filled with makeup and nail polish.

Once her basket was filled with colorful products, we checked out and kept our disguises in place on our quick walk back to the diner. We almost made it home with the goods when I noticed a huge dog hanging around my back door.

"Uncle Nick, do you know that dog?"

"Nope, stick close to me okay? I'm not sure if he's friendly." I shifted my body so Ruth was closer to the building and I stood between her and the dog.

"He has a collar, we should see if we can find his home." Ruth pointed out.

The dog barked and stood in front of Fox's door, staring

right at us. "Easy, buddy. We're just trying to get home." The dog trotted up to us lazily. "Who do you belong to?"

I held out my hand and let him sniff. Once he was done he sat at my feet and stared, waiting for me to make the next move. Leaning down slowly, I reached for his collar to find no tag on it.

"There's nothing on the collar." I stood up. "Let's go set this stuff inside and we can get him some water, he's probably been out here a while."

"We can take him home!"

"Your dad definitely wouldn't like that, Ruthie. But it's a nice idea." I reached for the door handle and led Ruth in first before the dog swiftly walked in behind her. Squirming his way past my legs, he trotted through the backroom and to my office.

"Jesus Christ." I darted for the dog, but he laid down next to my office chair and stared helplessly. He had full on 'Arms of the Angels' eyes. I stared at the ceiling while debating my next move.

A dog in the back of my diner was not a good look, but he was in the office and nowhere near any food. He clearly was looking for shelter or else he wouldn't have been on the street like that.

Ruth reached out and gently petted the dog's back end. "Can we keep him?"

"No, we can't keep him." Those eyes stared back at me again. "Maybe he could hang out with us for a few hours and I can drop him off at the vet after I take you home?"

Ruth's ponytail bobbed enthusiastically. "Yes, he can join Nick and Ruth day!"

An hour later and I had a ponytail in my hair and half of my fingernails painted messily with a mixture of pink and blue.

Ruth was going full out with my 'makeover', and I would have lied if I said I wasn't having fun.

"Hold still, let me add some pink cheeks to you too." I told her.

Ruth had bows clipped into her hair and I leaned in to carefully brush on pink to her cheeks. "It's called blush, Uncle Nick."

"Right, blush."

Scooby had laid down on the floor quietly during the entirety of our makeover. Before we started, I gave him a water bowl and a bit of chicken, but he wasn't interested. Ruth came up with the name and I applauded her for her creativity.

An alarming knock sounded at my back door. Followed by Fox's voice yelling, "Reid!"

I gently set down the play makeup and moved Ruth out of the way so I could rush to the back door. I swung it open hastily to be met with a frazzled Charlotte.

"What's wrong?" She stood frozen and continued staring at me. "Hello? Are you okay? Did something happen?"

She slowly breathed in a huge breath before bending over and laughing hysterically. "What the fu-"

Oh. My makeover. "Listen, do you need help or not?"

Her posture straightened and her smile made my frown lighten up a little. A strand of hair fell out of her messy ponytail and I wanted to push it back behind her ear. She covered her smile with her hand and I moved to grab her wrist and push it back down.

That action sobered her up a little, but the smile remained. Ruth showed up behind one of my legs. "Hi, Fox."

The woman in front of me bent down a little to say hi back to Ruth before looking between us. Her face returned back to the frantic look she had when I first opened the door. "I lost my dog. And I know you two are clearly busy with-" her hand gestured to my face. "This, but I've looked everywhere and I can't find him."

I blinked at her. Since when did Charlotte Fox have a dog? She could barely take care of her damn self after all the work she was doing for the cafe. Before I could even ask, another figure showed up on the opposite side of my legs as Ruth.

He bound up to Fox and jumped so his hind legs were on the ground while his front paws pressed into her stomach. She took a few steps back, but thankfully caught herself. "Link!" Her smile returned in full force.

She awkwardly petted the dog's head, and let him put his paws back on the ground. He wagged his tail happily and stood leaning against her while she looked back to me. "He was in your restaurant?"

Ruth answered before I could. "His name is Scooby!"

"You stole my dog?" Fox directed the question at me.

"Since when did you even have a dog? No, we didn't steal him, he was hanging around outside and barged in after us."

Her head tilted in that adorable puppy dog look I loved when she was thinking about something. She bent down to continue petting 'Link'. "You really do have a knack for crime don't you?"

When she stood up, she started laughing again. I rolled my eyes the best I could manage while not breaking into my own smile at how beautiful she was. "Ruth and I need to get back to our makeover now."

"You should join us. We can give you blush and some bows too." Ruth pointed to one of the sparkly pink bows hanging in her hair.

Charlotte's eyebrows raised as she looked to me for confirmation. Her smirk told me no matter what my opinion was, she was definitely going to be a witness to the rest of this makeover. I made a mental note not to let her take any pictures.

"Let me just put Link away, and I'll come over to help you out with this makeover. Sound good, Ruth?"

Ruth happily nodded and gave Link one last pet goodbye. Closing the door on that beautiful smile felt impossible, but I did it anyway with my best annoyed face. Hearing her laugh after it shut made it totally worth it.

"Do you like Fox, Uncle Nick?" Totally, kid.

How the hell did Ashton approach this subject with her? "Yeah, Ruthie. I do like her." We walked back to my office and I picked up the makeup again to finish my work on her cheeks. "What do you think about her?"

"She's really cool. She makes great sandcastles, she has a dog, and Georgia said they got tattoos together. I wonder if Fox would show me hers. Georgia has a peach." Ruth closed her eyes even though the brush I was using went nowhere near them. "Oh, and she's making a bookstore! That is very cool."

My heart warmed at her approval. I had never thought about how much it meant to me that my family liked Fox as much as I did. Never once in the past had I gone out of my way to introduce my family to anyone I was interested in. But then again, Fox wasn't like anyone else.

"It is pretty cool, isn't it?" We sat in silence as I continued my work until Charlotte snuck in through the back door.

I watched out of the corner of my eye as she crossed her arms and popped her hip and tilted her head to lean against the doorframe. When the pink heart I was drawing on the apple of Ruth's cheek was finished, I turned to give Fox my full attention. Nearly breathless after finding her there, looking like she belonged in my restaurant with a teasing smile on her face, I smiled.

"Ready for your turn in the hot seat?" I stood up and motioned for her to sit down.

Expecting her to bow out and just watch, she shocked me when she sat down and looked at Ruth. "Make me over please."

Ruthie's sweet smile made my heart squeeze again as she started digging through the hair accessories we bought to find the perfect one for Fox's ponytail. She found a sparkly blue one that matched one of hers and stretched up to clip it onto the top of Fox's head.

"Well, how do I look? Can I pull off a bow?" Charlotte turned to me and did an adorably awkward pose showing off her new accessory.

My smile was so big it hurt. "Looks great, Fox."

Ruth clapped and started going for makeup while I watched the two interact. By the time Fox's makeover was over, my eyes were fully glazed over and my cheeks were sore from smiling so damn much.

Pulling out her phone, Charlotte assessed her new makeover in her camera after Ruth announced she was finally done. "Wow, I have truly never looked better. The pink eyeshadow was definitely a good call."

"And we match!" Ruth pointed to her bow and then got in frame of Charlotte's camera.

"Do you wanna take a picture together?" Charlotte asked and Ruth's hair bows bounced all over the place as she nodded.

They took a quick selfie before Ruth had one of her famously great ideas. "Uncle Nick, come take one with us!"

Fox's smile was award winning, and from that second I knew I would never escape this picture. It would live in infamous memory for the rest of my damn life.

But I took it anyway. "Where do you want me?"

We all resituated so that Ruthie sat on my lap while Charlotte and I sat next to each other with our sparkles and colorful makeup on proud display. "Say cheese!"

Fox snapped the picture and we all took a moment to analyze it. My hair looked like a wreck with a tiny lopsided ponytail plus a few rogue curls sticking up, and my messy pink and blue nails were visible as I pretended to pinch Ruth's cheek. Ruthie's smile made her look like the happiest kid on the planet, but my makeup skills made her look like a reject from clown camp.

Charlotte's head was tilted toward mine and her huge smile matched mine and Ruth's. Her sparkly blue bow proudly sat on top of her head and her sparkly eyes and cheeks were as bright as the sun. She had a hilariously red tipped nose on top of it, but she still looked like the most beautiful person I had ever seen.

Helping Ruth off my lap, I stood up and turned to Fox. "Will you send that to me?"

"If you want blackmail, you're going to have to do better. I look good," she said happily as she zoomed in on the picture to get a better look.

I snorted. "Just send it to me, will you?" Fox rolled her eyes, but sent it to me anyway.

From a distance, I heard my brother's voice and inwardly groaned. Ashton was probably my third favorite person on the planet, but his arrival meant he was taking away Ruth. Who happened to be one spot higher on that totem pole.

He bound around the corner and took in the scene before him, switching his focus between me and Ruth. I counted down until he burst out laughing ten seconds later. Fox stood up and joined us while Ash nearly collapsed on the floor from his obnoxious laughter.

Ruth reached out her hand to him. "What do you think, daddy?"

He wiped a rogue tear from the corner of his eye. "You look stunning, pop tart. What did you do to Uncle Nick?"

"I made him pretty." Ruth turned back to give me a proud once over.

Ash leant down and hugged her. "You sure did, didn't you?"

His eyes then turned to Charlotte. "You look pretty good too, Fox. Looks like you three had a good time."

My good mood soured a little at the mention of my nickname for her. It bothered me a little earlier when Ruth said it, but now I found myself full on glaring at my brother. Ruthie didn't know any better. Ashton sure as hell should know better.

"Thanks, I might have crashed their little makeover, but I'm not sorry for it. Ruth here has some serious talent." Charlotte looked a little flushed as she awkwardly formed her words.

Ashton nodded with a ridiculous smile on his face. He narrowed his gaze at me and his smile turned into a smirk. "Well, it was nice seeing you again, *Charlotte.* It's time for us to go, but we'll be seeing you again soon hopefully."

She nodded quickly. "Right, sounds good to me."

I leaned down and gave Ruthie a goodbye hug and kissed her cheek. "See you soon, Ruthie. I won't be as pretty the next time you see me."

She giggled and took her dad's hand. "Bye, brother," I said far more grumpily than I needed to.

As my family left, I turned back to Charlotte, who was taking stock of the things I kept in my office. She looked over my calendar covered in blue ink, and lowered herself to sit at my desk chair before sighing. "I need an office like this. Right now, it's just an empty coat closet with a laptop."

"I can help you get one set up if you'd like." She rolled around in the office chair. Then she turned back to my desk to start inspecting my overflowing cup of pens. "I keep one from each restaurant I work at."

Her eyebrow rose and she slid her eyes back to me. "Really?" I nodded. "I had no idea you were so sentimental."

"That's only the start of it, Fox."

She blinked before turning back to my computer. I watched her continue turning her head to look at my corkboard filled with reviews pinned up, but her head quickly shifted back to the computer screen.

"What's this?"

"What?"

She grabbed the mouse and clicked to open up the excel spreadsheet to cover the entire screen. I totally forgot I named it 'Fox's Food Ratings'. "You keep a record of all of the foods I've tried?"

"Yeah, I wanted to keep it all handy in one place." I started picking at one of my fingernails. Surely she wouldn't read it all.

Her posture straightened as she leaned in close to the computer screen. Well there goes all hope of not being embarrassed. She scrolled through the sixty three recipes I'd had her try since she'd been back in town, and my heart nearly stopped when she started reading the comments next to each of the ratings.

"Apparently I said your steak was too oddly shaped to deserve a full ten stars." She swiveled the chair to face me again.

My foot tapped on the tiled floor. "Yeah, harsh critic."

She stared at me as I felt like ripping out my fingernails. "I just felt like I needed a challenge, I wanted to see what dishes you rated highly."

"Right, because I'm the ultimate food critic."

"You are, I haven't achieved a full ten yet," I said genuinely.

She scoffed. "These critiques are totally bogus. I said your potatoes would have more of a wow factor if they were purple."

The memory brought a small smile to my face. "They're entirely valid. And I don't want the ten until I've earned it."

"All of your food is a ten, you moron. I was just playing along with your silly game."

I leaned in closer and tucked a stubborn piece of hair behind her ear. "It's not a silly game, Fox. I take my food very seriously."

Her eyes rolled and her lips curved into a pretty smile. So close to leaning in and kissing the shiny lip gloss off of her lips, I straightened when I heard my name being called. Jace rounded the corner and managed to hold his tongue when he saw our appearances.

"Hey, boss. Someone out front is here to see you about catering a business meeting."

Blowing out a shallow breath, I nodded. "Be right there."

"And Nick?"

"Yes."

"You might want to wipe off the eye makeup. The guy is wearing a suit."

My hand raised to pull the ponytail out of my hair and I

threw it at him as he walked off laughing. I turned to Fox and her pretty smile still remained. "Well, that's my cue. Time to go home."

I nodded. "Want me to walk you over?"

Her laugh rang a bell in my mind that sent serotonin flooding through my body. "It's about five steps. I'm sure I'll manage."

She began walking toward the back door and I followed her anyway. Counting the steps, I confirmed it was exactly six to go from my door to hers. Close behind her, I reached for her back door before she could and opened it wide for her to walk through. Those pretty green eyes rolled, and she fixed me with a stare.

"Thank you for your services, Pinky Pie." Her thumb reached up to rub some of the blush off my cheek.

I gently grabbed her wrist before putting it by her side. "Lock it behind me, please."

She nodded and I heard the lock click before walking away to go scrub my face the best I could.

18

Charlotte

The local florist was not someone I visited often. A dainty bell chimed as I walked into Roses and Vine, and I was hit with the smell of fresh flowers. Color filled every inch of the shop with tables and counters covered in various flowers and bouquets. Feeling a little overwhelmed, I walked up to the cash register and waited for help.

A woman with silvery gray hair and prominent smile lines greeted me. "Hey, I'm not sure what I'm looking for and was hoping you could help."

The woman nodded and put down the bundle of fresh cut roses she was carrying. "What can I help you with, dear?"

Originally I was going to go with plain roses, but now I suddenly felt it was important to make sure I got the exact kind of flowers that I needed. Looking around the shop, I debated how best to word the question without being depressing. Then a thought occurred to me, I memorized plenty of people's coffee orders by heart, I wondered if this woman had the same talent.

"Did you know Evangeline?" Her warm smile calmed my erratic nerves.

She walked around the counter and I followed her as she led me through the shop. "She was a wonderful lady, and a good friend." I suddenly felt a little silly, of course they knew each other. They ran businesses on the same street for years. "Peonies. She said they reminded her of her granddaughter, their blooms are transformative. The same flower can look unrecognizable in only a matter of days."

My feet glued to the floor as I listened to her speak. She told her friends about me? After a pointed look, I gathered that this woman knew exactly who I was. "Is there a particular color?"

"I think an assortment of colors will do nicely." She gathered a handful of flowers and I followed her helplessly as she weaved through the store with purpose. With various tiny and big flowers added to the bundle, she walked to the only clear table in the store and began arranging a bouquet. "Just this one bouquet, dear?"

I nodded and watched her work. The smile never left her face as she carefully placed each and every flower into the bundle tactfully. A normal person would probably make small talk, but I wasn't feeling very chatty at the time.

She finished up and I got out my wallet to pay, but she just waved me off. "For a friend." The vase she put the flowers in was a simple glass vase and the flowers really stole the show. I didn't recognize any of the other flowers she added in there, but it really was a breathtaking bouquet.

"I really don't mind paying," I insisted. Her head shook and she smiled at me with a beautifully sad look on her face. "What if I treat you to coffee or books instead?"

Her hand reached up to hold her necklace. "That sounds wonderful, I haven't worked myself up enough to come visit the cafe to check on you. I'm so sorry for that."

I totally understood the feeling of avoiding difficult things. "Well whenever you're ready, come on by. We open on September 1st, in just a few days. It's quite different now, I painted one of the walls, and the tables and chairs are new. Bookshelves take up most of the place, but I made sure to leave parts of her in it too."

A rogue tear fell from her cheek before she could wipe it away. Feeling like I was the one who needed to comfort her now, I asked, "What kind of coffee do you like?"

"I was never much of a coffee drinker, I prefer vanilla chai tea."

"Then I'll have to make one for you sometime." I gestured to the flowers and spoke, "Thank you again for these, it means a lot."

Her gentle smile and wave sent me on my way and I was off to do something that I had avoided for way too long. The drive over felt much longer than twenty minutes. When I put the car in park, I sat still for a while, just watching the birds and the trees moving in the wind. The place was peaceful, and Evangeline would have loved it.

Getting out of my car, I made my way around the cemetery and walked through, line by line until I found her name. There in the lush green grass, my grandmother's headstone sat with a couple of roses that had been there for a while. A flash of guilt hit me over the fact that others had visited her when I hadn't.

A heavy breath of air fell from my lips and I sank to my knees on the ground. Reaching up, I placed the vase of flowers next to her gravestone and moved to sit with my legs crossed. Wind picked up my hair and blew it all over the place as I stared at the contrast between the bright flowers and the dull gray stone.

My head turned to make sure we were completely alone before I started speaking, "So, we both know I'm not great at this whole talking thing."

I picked at blades of grass as I figured out what I wanted to say to her. There was so much to talk about. "I'm reopening the cafe soon, I gave it a bit of a makeover so I hope that's okay with you. It's beautiful, I renamed it to Brewing Pages and now we're going to sell coffee *and* books."

"I kept that flowery wallpaper that you loved. But I did get rid of those metal tables, they weren't very comfortable, so I hope you're not mad at me for that." A firetruck passed us with its sirens on and I turned to watch it go.

"Reid has been very helpful, I feel like you're secretly rooting for that to turn into something aren't you?" I laughed at the thought. If she were here, she would definitely be plotting some scheme for us to get stuck together and fall in love. "And I have a dog now, his name is Link. He's good company to have around since you're not here."

The wind picking up made the flowers in the bouquet rustle around a little. "I met your friend today." I cursed myself when I realized I didn't even ask for her name. "The florist? She was very nice, and she seems to miss you a lot."

"Sorry for talking your ear off. I just wanted to say goodbye, you know, since we haven't gotten to really do that yet." A sigh escaped my lips and I closed my eyes tightly to hold back tears. "Thank you, for everything. You saved my life, and I'm so grateful to you."

My throat tightened painfully as tears started flowing down my cheeks. "You're the best person I've ever met, and I hope that I can be half as loving as you are one day." My hands wiped at my cheeks harshly. "I'm doing my best, and I know you would be happy with that."

A shaky breath escaped me as I stood up. "I'll be back to visit, and I'll tell you how the reopening goes. I just wanted to say thank you again."

I hurriedly walked back to my car and fell into the seat while slamming the door shut. My head fell forward to rest against the steering wheel and I sat there for a long time letting out every tear that I had in me. Taking a deep breath when I was done, I decided my next plan of action and put the keys in the ignition.

* * *

The nearest big box gardening center was about thirty minutes out of town. I pulled into the parking lot with puffy cheeks and a mission. Finding a nice enough worker, I told him my project and he walked me through everything that I would need. I checked out with a giant rolling cart filled with dirt and various tools that the guy suggested.

Back at home, I put Link on one of his longer leashes and brought him outside with me. There were two giant gardening boxes in front of Brewing Pages, but to my knowledge they had never been used. I tied Link to a bike post nearby and started emptying the boxes that were filled with dried out dirt and pine straw.

Lugging bags of dirt back and forth from my car to the front of the store was not easy, but I did my best to make it work. My cute new gardening gloves that were originally purple were now black from the fresh soil as I emptied it into the containers that sat under my windows.

My jeans stretched as I crouched on the ground and started evening out the soil. I definitely wasn't dressed appropriately for this activity, but it wasn't like I had any overalls lying around. The hot sun beat down on us, and I took a quick break to get a bowl of water for Link. He was lucky enough to have a spot in the shade by the door, while I was left in the heat.

When I came back with a bowl of water, I found Reid crouching down and petting my dog. Link definitely loved the attention because his tail was swinging back and forth in long strides. He usually only wagged his tail like that for me. I took in the scene before interrupting it when I opened the door.

Both Reid and Link glanced up at me and I set down the bowl I was holding. "I had no idea you were into gardening. You look like Martha Stewart." His hand reached up to wipe at my forehead and his hand was left with a streak of dirt when he took it away.

"It's a new project I'm working on." Right now, it looked like a big pile of dirt and trash, because that's exactly what it was. Frustrated, I sat back down and started leveling out the second gardening box, so I could start planting the bulbs.

Reid sat down on the sidewalk next to me. "You're planting flowers?"

I nodded and reached for the package with bulbs to reread the instructions on the back. "Yeah, peonies."

"Do you want help?" he asked softly.

My head snapped up to look at him. I had been focusing on the project so much I was barely focused on his questions. "Oh, yeah. If you want to."

He gave me a sweet smile and took the instructions from my

hands. "Yeah, I do."

Leaning over his shoulder to also read, I added, "So there are pictures for those that can't read properly. I know you athletes can struggle a bit with big words."

He pinched my side and I gasped dramatically. "I can read just fine, Fox. You're the one that's making a mess with all of this dirt lying around. Maybe you should've asked for my help sooner."

A teasing smile was on his lips and he kept his eyes focused on the instructions. My hand swiped his cap so it flew off his head. I snatched it up and put the black baseball hat backward on my own head.

"Breaking and entering, and now stealing. No wonder Link has the tendency to commit crime." He met my eyes and admired his hat on my head before opening the pack and grabbing bulbs out.

We finished planting the flowers in the soil before I went to go fill up the watering can that I bought. Reid helped me clean up the mess I made with soil everywhere, and when we were done, I collapsed onto the sidewalk.

"My back hurts, gardening is no joke," I whined.

Link got up and ran over to me to check and make sure I was okay. He sniffed at my cheek as I scratched behind his ear and patted his back. "I'm good buddy, just tired."

"Does he like to fetch?" Reid asked.

My head tilted and I looked from Reid to Link. "Honestly, I don't know. We've never tried it."

He blinked at me before offering, "Do you want to take him to the park?"

I looked down to Link and his happy tail wagging. "Sure, I'll go grab some of his toys."

We piled in Reid's car to go on a short drive to the park. Apparently he kept a blanket in his car, he pulled it out and laid it on the grass for us to sit on. We were in a secluded corner, so Reid took off Link's leash and tested out his fetch abilities with a rope.

The rope went far and landed in a patch of pine straw near the treeline. I was sitting close to Reid on the blanket and watched Link stare at his toy fall, he turned back to Reid with a questioning look on his face. I burst out laughing at his expression. The poor dog must have thought this man was an idiot.

Link sat down on the blanket with us while Reid tried to encourage him to go get the toy with his words. I just patted my pup on the back, he was too smart for a silly game of fetch. Eventually, Reid stood up to go get the rope for him.

"Why don't you try his pig next? He seems to like that toy more than the others," I suggested.

Reid stood and threw the pig a shorter distance this time. Link grumbled and moved to lay down on top of me. I laughed again and watched as Reid went to go fetch the toy. Still determined, he came back and started shaking the toy around for Link to grab.

Out of nowhere, Link stood up and pounced on the toy. He playfully stole it from Reid and walked it back over to me and plopped it in my lap. "Throw it!" Reid called.

I threw it in his direction and Link sprinted after the toy. Excited to see my lazy dog playing for the first time, I laughed and cheered Reid on as they played tug of war over it. We ended up playing a game of monkey in the middle, where Reid and I threw the pig back and forth and let Link try to catch it midair.

Reid ended up fetching a lot more than Link did, but the park day was definitely a successful outing. When the two were done running around, they joined me on the blanket and laid down to catch their breath.

"Did you have fun?" I asked.

He breathed out a laugh and put his hand behind his head. "Yeah, he's a great dog. Not so great at fetch though."

I chuckled and took off his hat so I could lay down too. Setting it on Reid's stomach, I sighed and bent my knees while looking at the clouds. "I should probably give that back to you. Wouldn't want you to be without your favorite possession."

"It looks better on you anyway," he responded.

My eyebrows raised and I turned my head to look at him. His smile made me return it with my own. "You're such a dork."

"Whatever you say, Fox."

We enjoyed the sunshine and peaceful park until Link stood up and made it clear he was ready to go home. Reid dropped us off at my back door, and leaned in close as he was saying goodbye. "I'll see you soon, right?"

I nodded with my eyes on his lips. Everytime he invaded my space like this I forgot how to think. How to breathe, even. "Soon."

He stayed for a few seconds longer before backing up and waiting for me to close my door. I softly closed and locked it before trudging over to my laptop to finally start working for the day.

19

Charlotte

My pillowcase felt damp underneath my head as I moved to push a wet strand of hair out of my face. All night my mind kept wandering back to Reid, no matter how much I tried to focus on work. Researching how to market a bookstore in a small town was nowhere near as interesting to my mind as Nicholas Reid.

Finally giving up hope for being productive, I decided to take a shower and lay down to try and sleep off these thoughts. He was just so kind, and confident in himself. I had never met anyone else like Reid, but he felt familiar, like a home I once knew and somehow forgot about.

Nothing on my phone was interesting, so I slapped it down on the bed and stared at the wood paneled ceiling of my loft. I counted twenty planks before picking up my phone again and pulling up Reid's name. We had no message history whatsoever. A perfectly blank slate.

My eyes squeezed shut and I opened them to type quickly. 'Hey, are you busy?'

I hit send before I could even second guess myself. A blue message stared back at me as I waited for a response. Crickets chirped outside and a faint glow from the streetlamp streamed in my dimly lit loft while I waited for a bubble with three dots to pop up on my phone.

'No, do you want me to come over?' Absolutely.

'If you're not busy.'

Through the wall that separated our buildings, footsteps bounding down stairs were audible before a loud crash, so I decided to get off my bed and meet him at my back door. While quick, I was nowhere near as fast as Reid. By the time I hit the bottom of my stairs, a key was jiggling in the lock and the door swung open to show a very tall and handsome friend of mine.

"Hey." He awkwardly rested his hand along the side of the doorframe. Unfamiliar with this unconfident Reid, I decided to take the safe route.

"Hey," I replied. The sleeves of my sweatshirt covered my hands as I pulled at them nervously. It was the middle of the night, and I invited Nicholas Reid into my apartment. What the hell was I supposed to do next?

Thankfully my trusty pup was there to break the tension. Link bound up to us and sniffed his hand. "Come in, we don't want him to escape."

Reid followed my orders and closed the door behind him. He bent down to give Link a little extra attention before looking up at me through his eyelashes. "You look comfy."

My gaze fell down to my outfit. A pink volleyball sweatshirt covered my top half, and my tiny pajama shorts covered in bananas left more to be desired in the fashion department. "Yeah, I was going to go to bed, but I couldn't sleep."

He nodded and waited for me to continue. "Do you want to come upstairs?"

"Yeah, I would like that." His dark eyes were open and as pretty as ever. God, I was so jealous of those damn eyelashes.

We turned to start walking up and I pointed to Link's bed at the entrance to the cafe. "You stay down here, okay?"

My pup slowly trotted to his bed, laying his head on his paws before giving me pitiful puppy dog eyes. I couldn't help my smile before waving at him. "Good night."

Then I turned to find an odd expression that I didn't recognize on Reid's face. Quirking an eyebrow, I led the way up the stairs with him following close behind.

"So- what were you up to before I interrupted?" I stammered. My brain was empty. In the twenty something years of practice that I had conversating, somehow it vanished in less than a minute.

He chuckled and I prepared myself for him to comment on how I was acting like an unsocialized cave woman. "Not much I-"

My foot caught on the top stair and in slow motion I saw my hands raise to protect my face from falling flat on the hardwood. Thankfully a strong set of arms wrapped around my waist and caught me before I fell all the way to the floor. Once I was stable, I pushed up on my fingertips to right myself.

"Thanks," I breathlessly offered. My inner monologue filled with any curse word under the sun that I could think of.

Reid just stood there, staring at me with a bewildered smile. "You're acting awfully strange tonight, Fox."

I tucked a damp piece of hair behind my ear. "Yeah, agreed," I whispered.

He stepped closer to me and untucked my hair, twirling

the strand as his fingers slowly slid down it. "Your invitation shocked me."

"It did?"

"Yeah, I didn't know we were the kind of friends that hung out in the middle of the night."

My face was on fire and I was half tempted to pull up my hood and tighten the strings until I suffocated in the fabric. I raised my hand to do just that, but he stopped me. His hand held my wrist and I found myself admiring his confident smile.

"I'm only teasing, Fox." He muttered with that dumbly pretty smirk on his lips.

I swatted at his hand holding my wrist, but he didn't let go. His grip loosened, but instead of dropping it, he trailed his touch all the way up to my shoulder before wrapping his hand gently around the nape of my neck. My breathing shallowed and I focused on being as quiet as possible.

Remembering it was my turn to respond, I nodded. That was the best I could manage with those dark eyes so close to mine and his nose bumping into mine softly. My eyes flicked down to his lips and back up to those eyes that seemed to sparkle when they looked at me.

Everything slowed down as he leaned in even closer. My heart stopped in my chest, and I forgot how to breathe when his lips touched mine. He was soft and sweet. Instantly feeling emotional, I tried to shove down my feelings as he kissed me like he worshiped me.

His hand on my neck was comforting and his thumb wrapped around to brush right under my ear. Totally over-whelmed with the feeling of Reid, I felt myself relaxing. The kiss continued slowly until he ultimately backed away. Entire worlds could have been made and destroyed in the time that kiss went on and I would have been none the wiser.

Pulling back, his hand slid away from my neck to rest on the small of my back. His eyes searched mine and he smiled sweetly, which I supposed meant he liked what he saw. "Was that what you were hoping for when you invited me over?"

"Would that be a bad thing?" I whispered, still staring at his lips. My admission made the smile take over his face.

"Not in the slightest."

A hand on my waist, he pulled me in close again and kissed me with more force this time. My brain finally turned on and I returned his passion in full. It had been months since I had been with someone. And I had never felt so much tension with anyone in my life.

I wanted Nicholas Reid.

His hands weaved through my hair tightly and his arms pulled me into him impossibly closer. Sighing into the kiss, I moved to feel his ridiculously big arms that I had been admiring for the past month while he carried heavy objects for me. They felt just as good as they looked.

A tinge of pain bloomed in my lip as he bit down on it playfully. Shocked, I moved to meet his eyes and teasing smile. He gave me a few seconds to stare before moving to kiss behind my ear and down my neck. I let out a low moan without meaning to and he chuckled while stepping between my legs and forcing me to walk backward.

Backing me all the way to my new fluffy sofa, he pushed until I bounced down on the oversized cushions. He looked down at me for a moment before lowering to his knees on the floor in front of me. Parting my legs wide, he moved between them and reached for my sweatshirt.

"Mind if I take this off?" My head shook before he even

finished his sentence.

It was ripped up and over my head in a flash. Reid tossed the sweatshirt to the side carelessly as he took in the sight in front of him. "Do you always wear nothing underneath these?"

I thought back to the few times he had seen me in sweatshirts in the past. Summer was just ending, so I really only wore them at night time when I wanted to make myself comfy. "I hate the feeling of wearing layers. Sometimes I wear a bra."

His eyes darkened as his mind clearly went on a trip picturing that image, so I sat and waited. When he rejoined me back on planet earth, he reached up for my jaw and pulled me into him again. I melted into his touch as his hands felt their way up my stomach to cup my boobs.

He gave a gentle squeeze and teasingly bit down on my lip again before showing his attention to my tits. I gasped as he licked at my nipple, and I felt my body flush. My back arched into him and he pulled my body up onto the very edge of the couch so he could get closer.

"You are so fucking beautiful." His thumb rubbed over my nipple slowly, his eyes watching it harden under his touch. Those dark eyes flicked up to meet mine and he murmured, "The most beautiful thing I have ever seen."

My heart stopped again and my body tensed. Being like this with Reid felt like I was wide open on display and he could easily stick his hand in and rip my heart out if he so desired. My nervousness was quickly pushed to the side by my desire as he returned his attention to my nipple.

I pulled him up by the back of his neck and started kissing him again when I felt the emotion become too much. Just like before, his lips made my worries melt away. I kissed him forcefully, like I was scared he might change his mind if we went too slow.

Then he backed away again. Both hands sliding down to my embarrassingly dorky sleep shorts, he slipped the tips of his fingers in the waistband. "I'm gonna take these off now, Fox." His voice was deep and intense and I felt my pussy clench.

Though his hands didn't move until I answered, "Yes, please."

He seemed quite satisfied with my manners as he began pulling at them until they hit mid thigh. We both froze our movements when Link barked downstairs.

We paused and waited. Seconds passed and nothing, so Reid looked to me, and when I nodded he started pulling at them again. But then the faint sound of breaking glass stopped us.

Reid started tugging my shorts back up and pulled his shirt up and over his head to toss it at me. "Stay here."

He hurried toward the door to go downstairs as Link started barking angrily.

20

N ick

Even though I told Fox to stay upstairs, she still followed me down. The only object that I saw in the back of her store that could protect us was a giant umbrella, so I grabbed it and continued walking. Link's barking covered any sound of the intruder which made it hard to tell what to expect.

I stood next to the doorway that led to the front of her shop and waved at Charlotte to stay back. She lowered her eyebrows in frustration, but seemed like she was going to stay in place. Umbrella in hand, I popped up around the doorway and immediately saw a motherfucker in all black.

Link had him backed up against the front door with his hands held up to placate the dog. The only weapon I saw was a hammer in one of his raised hands, so I continued moving forward and yelled, "What the *fuck* are you doing here?"

As I got closer I saw shards of glass reflecting moonlight and a small portion of the window next to Fox's door broken, so he could turn the lock and let himself in. I also recognized the man and nearly skewered him with the pointy tip of the umbrella.

"*Alex?*" Fox seethed from behind me.

He lowered his hands and stared between the two of us. Dressed in all black, he looked like one of the morons from Home Alone. Fox called Link over to her so he would stop barking.

Silence filled the room until I broke it loudly, "I'm going to ask you one more time. What the *fuck* are you doing?"

Never in my life had I gotten into a physical fight with anyone other than my brother, and that was when we were kids. But if this fool thought he could break in and hurt my girl, he was sorely fucking mistaken. I would put a dent in his head before he even got close to her.

"Look man-" He started stuttering, but I interrupted to knock the hammer out of his hand. I yanked him by the back of his shirt and shoved him against the nearest wall.

Behind me, I heard Charlotte quietly talking and looked to see she was no longer in my eyesight. I hoped to God she was calling the police. "Listen, I have been trying to contact her and she was giving me a hard time. You know how women are, man. She has something I need, all I'm trying to do is get my stuff back and I'll be on my way."

I shoved him into the wall one more time for good measure and then pointed to a chair. "Sit."

He looked to the chair and back to me. "Look, this is a bad time. I'll just go."

Trying to slip past my ironclad grip on his shoulder, he flinched when I squeezed harder. "Sit. You aren't fucking going anywhere."

Calling out to Fox, she told me she was on the phone with 911 and they would be here soon. She sounded disturbed and I had another flash of anger flood through my body. "You stay back there, okay honey? You can go upstairs if you want. I'll take care of this."

Watching the doorway, I didn't see her again as she said okay. I didn't hear footsteps either, so I assumed that meant she was standing or sitting on the other side of the wall. Needing to protect her outweighed my need to comfort her as I continued standing in front of the asshole. His eyes were getting shifty as he looked for a way to run past me.

He tried once before I grabbed his arm and slammed him back onto the chair, which made it loudly scrape across the floor. "You're fucking pathetic. If you ever even think about coming near her again, you'll wish you were never born."

"Look, she stole something from me. And I want it back. This is just as much her fault as it is mine!" His desperate voice pleaded. I watched his every movement as I paced quickly back and forth in front of him until the police arrived. Red and blue lights reflected inside the cafe. The policemen came inside and asked who I was and to explain the situation.

Noise flooded the cafe as police officers and detectives came in. A couple of minutes later, the asshole didn't deny my accusations and they were cuffing him. He looked scared shitless and the coward quietly walked out to the police car with his hands behind his back. I excused myself and went to go find Charlotte, who was sitting on the other side of the wall on the floor with Link laying across her legs.

Sinking down to the floor next to them, I pulled her into my lap the best I could with Link in the way. She tucked her head into the crook of my neck and slipped her arms around my waist. The sound of sobs wracking her body broke my heart into tiny pieces.

The police insisted on taking her down to the station and

getting a statement from Fox while tears still streamed down her cheeks. I did my best to wipe them away, but they wouldn't stop falling. She asked to change into clothes before leaving and the officers agreed.

I started up the stairs to follow her, but she turned and more tears started flowing from her eyes. "You need to stay with Link, or take him to the vet." She sniffled and took a deep breath to steady her words. "He's bleeding a little, I think he's got glass in his paw."

"You don't want me to go with you?"

She shook her head and insisted in that wobbly voice, "No, I promised to take care of him. And I can't right now, so I need you to please. You don't even have to take him to the vet, I just don't want him to be alone."

My heart fractured into even tinier pieces. "What if I called Ash or Georgia to go with you? Or they can stay with Link, Georgia loves animals."

She laughed pitifully and wiped more tears. "I'd rather do this alone, honestly. But thank you. I'm going to get changed."

When she returned downstairs she was clad in another baggy sweatshirt and sweatpants. Her hood was pulled up and all of her tears were dried with an emotionless expression on her face. I sighed and pulled her into my arms one last time before walking her to the police car.

"If you change your mind, call me and I'll be there in a second." She nodded and I pushed back a lock of her hair.

Turning to an officer, I asked how long they would be and he said it would be at least a few hours to finish filling out all of the paperwork and discussing her options. I waved goodbye and returned back inside to kneel down and check out Link.

After looking at all of his paws, he did have one cut, but I didn't see any glass in it. I fumbled around Fox's apartment looking for a leash to take him to an emergency vet. The situation could probably wait until morning, but I needed a distraction until Fox came home and I knew it would take stress off her plate if she knew Link was okay.

On our way out, the broken window caught my eye again. I told Link to sit away from the window while I swept up glass shards from the floor. Then I grabbed a roll of duct tape and covered the window as a temporary measure.

The emergency vet assured me Link was perfectly fine. They were kind enough to spray the wound with an antiseptic and wrap it up for me before I took him home. We rode with the windows down in silence on the way back.

I let Link into the cafe and we both returned to the main storefront to sit by the door and wait for Charlotte to return. He laid down on his giant dog bed and stared at the door with me. The gray duct tape reminded me to send a text to my friend, asking him if he could replace the small window first thing in the morning.

Despite the hour, he responded quickly and said he would be here at six. Out of productive things to do, I stood and began pacing across the length of the cafe. Link whined every now and then, so I sat next to him and pet him until he settled again.

"I know bud, I miss her too."

A cop car pulled up in front of the window and we both jumped to our feet. Fox got out of it and I opened the door, both Link and I stepping outside to run up to her. "You okay?"

She nodded and the officer waved to us before taking off. Her eyelids drooped and she looked zombie-like as we headed into the cafe and up to her apartment. "What happened?"

20

"He was arrested for breaking and entering with a weapon, and I filed a restraining order," she spoke softly. All emotion was devoid in her voice and face now.

I led her to the bed and had her sit down. "Are you comfortable? Do you want to change your clothes?"

Her head shook. "Okay." Doing my best to think of what would help her in this moment, I walked over to her freezer to find what I was looking for. It was totally empty. "Do you mind sitting here with Link for a minute while I go grab something?"

She still stared at the wall across from her as her head shook again. Then she turned to Link, when she saw a bandage on her paw I explained, "He's okay, I took him to the vet and they said he just needed a wrap and some antiseptic spray. It wasn't a deep cut, and no glass was in it."

"Good, I'm glad." Lifting a hand for him, Link jumped up on the bed and slid under her hand to accept pets.

"I'll be right back, Fox."

Out of breath when I returned, I ripped the plastic cover around the ice cream container and opened it. Pulling out a spoon from her silverware drawer, I handed both over to Fox. "Ice cream?"

She gave a small nod and grabbed both. "You keep rocky road?"

My small smile was strained. I wished this ice cream would come in handy during some other much happier situation, but I was still happy I had it. We sat in silence as she ate and I moved to turn off the harsh overhead light and leave a lamp on.

I nervously sat back on the end of the bed while she continued to eat in silence before stopping. "You done?"

She handed it to me and I put the ice cream in her freezer

and the spoon in the sink. Returning next to her I asked, "Do you want me to stay the night?"

Looking up at me with sadness filling her eyes she answered, "Yes, please."

I wrapped my arms around her and pulled her into a hug. I was thanking my lucky stars that she said yes. Otherwise, I imagined Link's dog bed downstairs would not have been too comfortable to sleep on all night.

Helping her off the bed, I pulled down the blankets and she slipped underneath them to lay down. The lamp light clicked off as I pulled on the string and then returned to the opposite side of the bed and slid in next to her. I should probably sleep on the couch, but something told me we both needed to be close to each other.

When I slid in she scooted closer and I took that as my signal to scoop her up in my arms. We stayed like that all night long, with her resting against me, her head nestled into my shoulder and my arms wrapped around her waist.

Eventually I fell asleep knowing that I would never sleep well again without her in my arms like this. Knowing Fox was comfortable enough with me to pass out on top of me was like giving my brain an all time high. I was an instant addict and would never be able to sleep soundly without her again.

21

Nick

My body naturally woke up before the sun rose as usual. Fox's face was quite a sight to wake up to, so I remained in place and watched her until a banging downstairs woke us. Checking my phone to see the time, I confirmed my suspicion and put it down to keep staring at Fox.

Her stunning eyes looked back up at me and the golden morning sunrise streaming through the curtains made her look like an angel with a halo of flyaways because of her bedhead. She blinked a few times before hiding her face in my neck.

I chuckled quietly and let her wake up slowly. When she lifted her face again, my gaze returned. Her voice was gritty as she spoke, "You have quite a staring problem."

"You're beautiful," My hand raised to push the hair that was covering half her face now. "And I have no problems."

Her cheeks flushed a little and she returned her head to rest on the pillow next to me. My hand found hers and I played with her fingers as I admired what she looked like when she

167

first woke up.

"Thank you for taking care of me," she mumbled.

"Always."

Her eyes met mine with a question lingering in them. Now was not the time to go into detail, so I didn't. I pulled our linked hands upward until I slid mine away and pushed hers to rest behind my neck.

I leaned in for a short kiss. Although clearly that was a terrible plan, because I could never kiss her for a short amount of time. She interrupted my gentle confession by pushing on my chest.

"I need to brush my teeth." My eyes rolled and I turned to lay on my back while she got up and walked to her bathroom.

Sitting up, I waited for her to return on the edge of the bed and watched Link mirror my actions from his spot on the floor. When she was done she came and sat right next to me. Sighing, I brushed more hair out of her face that was blocking my view and tucked it behind her ear.

She moved to rest her head on my shoulder and I wrapped my arm around her back to support her. We stayed like that for a while.

"Are you feeling better or worse today?" I asked.

Lifting her head from my shoulder, she looked at me before responding. "I'm not sure, but I don't want to talk about it right now."

"Okay, what do you want to do then?" She could ask to visit Antarctica and I would figure out how to make her a damn igloo.

She paused for a while, so I tried thinking of how to help. She said that she didn't know how she felt, so maybe that meant she also didn't know what to do. "What would you normally be doing if I wasn't here?"

Staring at me for a little longer, Charlotte nodded her head toward the bathroom. "My morning routine, and then probably walking Link."

I stood up and turned to offer her a hand to join me. She followed my lead and let me walk her into the bathroom. "Okay, what's first?"

"What do you mean?"

"How does your morning routine go?" Her cheek still had imprints from sleeping on my shoulder and her face turned into an adorable pout.

"Why? We can do something-" I interrupted her by slapping my hand on the counter behind her.

She just continued to stare at me with confusion, so I clarified, "Hop up, we'll do your routine together."

I could practically see the cogs turning in her brain as she decided to go along with my silly idea. Lifting herself up to sit on the counter, she parted her legs and turned to the products lining her bathroom mirror. She picked up a small white bottle and handed it to me.

Gently holding it, I tried to unscrew the cap. Charlotte laughed quietly at me and retook it from my hands to pop it off for me. I had no clue what the hell I was doing so I kept staring until she explained, "It's moisturizer. I usually do two pumps of it onto the tips of my fingers and pat it onto my face."

Stepping between her legs to get close to her face, I did as she said and put my fingers together until there was some product on both of my hands. Her face stayed perfectly still as she stared at me intensely. I broke our eye contact to start softly patting the moisturizer on her skin.

We were both quiet while I worked. I wasn't even sure if Fox was breathing, but I felt the weight of her gaze on me. "Am I doing this right?"

Her serious expression softened into a smile. "You're doing great," she said. Her voice was the softest I had ever heard it.

When I deemed my job done, she then handed me sunscreen to rub onto her face. I had never seen such a tiny bottle of sunscreen in my life. She bit her lip to hide a smile when I made sure to cover her ears and neck with the sunscreen too.

I had never been so close to anyone like this. All I was doing was putting silly named products on her face, but the way she was looking at me like I deserved the world made me want to melt into a puddle on the floor. Taking care of her in such an intimate way only made me fall more in love with her.

She handed me a serum to put on which involved some sort of dropper situation. I had no clue Fox woke up every morning putting tiny potions on her face, but maybe that was why she only looked prettier and prettier every day. When I fumbled with the bottle, she instructed me to hold out my hands and put a few drops on them so that I could put it on her face.

Her skin was glossy after all of the products were put on, and I returned my eyes to hers with a proud smile on my face. The tears in her eyes made me pause. "Are you okay? What's wrong?"

She moved to turn her head, but my hand lifted her chin to keep her attention. I repeated, "What's wrong?"

"Nothing, it's dumb," she whispered. I sighed and swept my thumb along one of her soft and shiny cheeks. "This is nice."

"You're crying because it's nice?" I asked.

She let out a wet laugh. "Yeah, I am." Her hand came up to hold mine while it still cupped her cheek. We stared at each other for a moment and her thumb rubbed mine lovingly.

"You're a real sap, Charlotte Fox." That earned me another beautiful laugh. "I think this is nice too, I like that you let me see you like this."

Her nod was quick and she let go of my hand. "The next thing on my list is my hair." Her hands gently pushed at my hips until I backed up enough for her to jump off of the counter. Turning to me with a brush held out, she let me take it and led me back to her bed.

"Are you sure you don't mind doing this? It's okay if you need to go."

I sat criss cross applesauce on the bed behind her. "Not at all, I really do like it." She gathered her hair and threw it all behind her so it laid against her back on display for me. It was beautiful, long, and unruly. "Besides, maybe this means I can get you to dye my hair one day."

That made her twist around until she could see my face. "Really?" When she saw I was serious she turned back around. "I would like that, Dyl let me dye her hair pink once and it was really therapeutic for some reason."

"To be clear, there won't be any colors involved."

She giggled and I started gently brushing through the ends of her hair. I was totally going to wake up with pink hair one of these days, but it was totally fucking worth it. Charlotte slouched as I brushed her hair and I felt her relax into me.

"I don't think anyone's ever touched me the way you do." Her confession startled me. My hands paused and then resumed their motion as I contemplated how to respond.

"What do you mean?" I had an idea of what she meant, but I wanted to hear her say it.

Her body became more rigid as we sat in silence after my question. She thought for a few moments before responding,

"Like you care about me, but deeper than that. It's like you genuinely want to take care of me without anything in return. Total selflessness."

She breathed out a breath before adding, "You're terrifying."

I couldn't help but chuckle a little at that. "I do care about you."

That ended our conversation and I finished brushing her hair until there were no more knots or hangups. I didn't want this to be over so soon, so I decided to braid her hair without breaking our quiet tension. Ruthie had taught me how to do this once, and I still had no damn clue what I was doing.

Charlotte stopped me after about fifteen minutes of fumbling around trying to tie her hair into a braid. "Are you trying to re-knot my hair?"

I gave a frown at my hopeless attempt. "No, I was trying to braid it." She laughed at me and pushed my hands away to untangle the mess that I put her silky dark hair in. The tension in the air was palpable as we stared at each other after sitting in silence for so long.

"Do you want to go to the diner and eat-" Fox interrupted me by leaning closer with her hand landing on my shoulder. She straightened to be able to reach my lips. Pulling me into a heated kiss, she quickly moved to shuffle herself in my lap with both of her legs over mine and our chests pushed together.

Gently cupping her jaw, I held her face still as I pulled mine away. "Fox, I don't know if this is a good idea." Her lips chased mine while I spoke.

"I've wanted this for so long, Reid. Please. This is what I want." Her lips forcefully locked with mine and I returned her passion in full.

Sliding my hands over her hips and under her ass, I turned

around to gently push her to lay flat on the bed. If this was what she wanted, that's what she would get. Returning my lips to hers, I kissed her roughly and tangled my fingers in her hair.

Fox shoved me back and stood up to undress. I watched her strip away every piece of her clothing until she stood before me completely naked. My hands shot up to feel her and I traced damn near every inch of her body that I could get my hands on while I kissed her again.

Her hands lifted to my pants and she unbuttoned them before yanking them down. The hem of my t-shirt was lifted next and I took that as my cue to take it off for her. We stood before each other, entirely vulnerable and she took advantage of my hesitation to shove me to sit on the bed.

Once again, she climbed into my lap and started kissing my neck. "Fuck, you are so goddamn pretty," I confessed while my hands grabbed at her ass.

I reached up with a hand to make a path down from her tits to her clit and I slowly tested her reaction. She was dripping wet, so I spread some of it from her hole to her clit. She grinded down into my hand, so I took that as my hint that she wanted more. I pushed her back to lay flat on the bed again and got down on my knees.

"Are you sure?" She looked shocked at my position.

I pushed one of her thighs to rest over my shoulder. "Yes, tell me what you like and don't, okay?"

She nodded hurriedly and I began slowly. I teased her with my tongue as her legs twitched and her ass raised to help my mouth find the spot where she needed me. Letting her direct me to where she wanted, I picked up the pace when she stilled her movements and entangled her fingers into my hair. Her whines came out as I continued with my slow pace. She tasted fucking delicious, and I was going to savor every damn second of this.

This was the woman of my dreams, and I would be damned if I didn't make her cum with my mouth before fucking her. Her legs started clenching and I felt her pulling harder on my hair, so I sucked on her clit until she hit her climax. She let out a string of cuss words before taking her hand out of my hair and instead pulling on the sheets underneath us. I groaned at the loss, but continued on, wanting to make her cum as hard as possible.

"Fuck, that was so fucking good, Reid." Her cheeks were pink and her hair was a mess against the bedsheets. I smiled at her praise and greeted her with a kiss. She kissed me back passionately, even with the taste of her on my lips.

"You ready for me?" I grabbed my hard cock and tapped it against her clit. Her body jumped and she pushed at my shoulder to give her space so she could sit up.

Pointing to the bed, she motioned for me to sit down. After slipping on a condom from my wallet, I leaned against the headboard with my legs out in front of me and she crawled over toward me. Nearly cumming at the sight of her tits hanging and her ass moving with her sexy crawl, I couldn't help but groan.

She laughed at my eagerness. "I haven't even done anything yet."

"You could literally stare at me while crawling toward me just like that, and I would cum for you," I said, being one hundred percent honest.

Her hands were placed on my chest and she swung one of her thighs over both of mine. "We'll have to try that some other time." Fuck yes, there would definitely be more of this happening.

My hands moved to her hips as she lowered herself down on my dick. Her whimper made my grip tighten on her and I held her still. "You okay?"

She nodded and pushed her forehead to rest on my shoulder. "You're too fucking big." I groaned at her words and my hips jutted up a little.

Giving her a minute to adjust, I tried to think of literally anything else other than her. She recovered quickly and kept sliding herself down on my cock. I looked down to see where she was taking me in and I nearly lost it at the sight of us together.

Her hips started moving, and she was riding me like a goddamn champ. Her breaths were quick as I slid a hand up behind her neck so she would look down at me. "You're taking me so fucking well, baby."

Her pussy clenched down on me at the words. That pretty mouth was hung open as moans spilled out of it, and I pulled her neck, so that she was even closer to kiss her. My tongue found its way into her mouth and I tasted her honey flavored chapstick while she rocked back and forth on my cock.

Hips stuttering as she grinded her clit against me while I was fully inside of her, I encouraged her to keep moving with my hands on her ass. She slowed down, but I knew she was getting close by the sounds of her pretty moans, so I held her hips still and started driving up into her until she collapsed into my arms and gave into her orgasm.

I followed her shortly after and we sat there in a sweaty mess for a bit. Our breathing quieted down and I squeezed her hip. "You okay, Fox?"

She nodded and gave me a look at her face. Her dopey smile was fucking phenomenal, and I almost forgot how to breathe again. I helped her off of me and laid her down on the bed before getting up to take off the condom and grab a towel to clean us up.

22

Charlotte

Floating on a cloud was the only way I could explain this feeling. Reid and I laid on our backs next to each other while we caught our breath. He turned his head to stare at me while the dreamy smile stayed in place on my face.

Only he could make me feel okay after something that was so awful happened. I pushed that thought to the back of my brain for the time being and turned to face him.

"You look happy," he mumbled while twirling a lock of my hair around his finger.

The serene look on his face coupled with sex hair made my head spin. "So do you." I turned back to the ceiling and tried my best to focus on keeping this feeling for the longest amount of time possible. "I feel floaty."

Reid snickered at my sappy comment and reached his hand over to flick my nose. It scrunched up at the offense, but before I could say anything he leaned in to kiss it. I waited for him to tease me for my words, and when he didn't, I relaxed back into bed and closed my eyes.

"Are you still sleepy?" he asked. He was fully on his side now and leaning over me.

I shook my head and opened my eyes to meet his. Looking down at his lips, I was more than ready for round two. He interrupted my fantasy with words. "Come on, let's get dressed."

"Dressed?"

He hummed in agreement. "You need breakfast, come on."

I changed into slightly less baggy clothes, following Reid into his diner and up to his loft. Declaring he needed a quick shower, he pointed to the bed for me to sit and I patiently waited while rummaging through his entire apartment. He never said I couldn't poke around.

On his side table sat pictures of him and Ashton, some of Ruth, and a few of all three of them together. There was also a collage I hadn't noticed before of what I assumed were pictures from his travels. They all looked wildly different and had no people in them, but the images held a personal touch that made me think Reid took them himself.

Noticing his phone on the kitchen counter, I tapped it to check the time and was met with the picture we took with Ruth after our makeover. He made me his screen saver. *Us.* I choked back emotion and decided to return to sitting quietly on the couch.

When he exited the bathroom, his eyes immediately found me. We shared lovesick smiles before he walked over and kissed me deeply. My hands ran through his wet curls. His hair was still relatively short, but it had grown out since I first came back to Rosewood and I loved it.

"I can dye it back if you want." He said as he stared at me

while I brushed through his hair.

"What?"

"My hair, you said you don't like it dark, so I can dye it whatever color you want."

My eyebrows furrowed as I tried remembering what the hell he was talking about. "I love your dark hair. When did I say that?"

"The second you walked back in town. You said 'Your life must have taken a dark path for you to get into hair dye.' Or something along those lines."

I smiled at his attentiveness to my words. "I love it dark. You should keep it." My hands ran through his hair one last time before I dropped them.

"Good to know." He nipped at my cheek and left me waiting as he headed downstairs. His tight black shirt drew my eye until my gaze trailed down to his dark blue jeans. Now that I knew what was underneath those clothes, it seemed criminal for the pants to be so ill fitting.

We took our usual positions, I sat on a barstool and he stood across from me behind the bar. "Pancakes or french toast today?"

I hummed while contemplating my options. "I want cinnamon roll french toast."

His confused expression was adorable. "A cinnamon roll and french toast?"

"Nope, cinnamon roll french toast."

"That's not a thing."

I sighed, pretending to be a disgruntled customer. "And here I was thinking that I was the food critic. It's a very exquisite dish, definitely worthy of fine dining, and possibly worthy of a full ten stars."

His eyes rolled and he waited for me to actually order. "Pancakes sound good."

Calling out my order, he then told me he was going to go to the back and check to make sure everything was running smoothly. The bell at the door drew my attention, I glanced over to see Georgia walking in. She gave me a wave and a sweet smile before sitting down next to me.

"Good morning, here for breakfast?" she asked. I nodded and returned her greeting. "I'm just picking breakfast up for Ash and Ruth. Apparently we have a big day planned."

"That's very exciting." Reid showed up again and dropped off my pancakes. He took Georgia's order and went back to help prepare it.

Georgia gave me a look and quietly added, "You two are getting good at that."

"Good at what?"

She leaned on her hands that were perched on the counter-top of the bar. "The fleeting glances and lovey dovey stuff. It's totally believable." Her smile told me she genuinely meant it. I remained silent while I tried to figure out what she was referring to. "Oh, Ash told me that you two were faking it until your ex got off your back. Was I not supposed to know?"

My eyebrows shot into my hairline as I processed her words. Right. We were totally faking it, and Reid told Ashton that. This was all fake. "Right, sorry. No, it's totally fine that you know. I mean, it's probably obvious."

Georgia's face fell and she held up her hands. "I wasn't trying to-"

I stood up and grabbed my keys before backing up. "I just realized I forgot to feed Link, I've gotta go." Calling out a quick goodbye over my shoulder, I hurried out of there and went home.

23

Nick

Practically dancing through the motions of assembling my family's breakfast order, I spun around with the to-go boxes in hand and walked out to give them to Georgia. When I returned to the bar, I found an empty barstool with a full plate of pancakes in one seat and a very guilty looking Georgia in the seat next to it.

"Where did she go?" I asked, handing her the bag.

She grimaced and grabbed the bag. "I said something dumb, and I don't know entirely what happened. But she seemed upset and went to go take care of Link."

My heart dropped in my stomach. "What did you say?"

Georgia's hands flailed around as she spoke, "Well Ash said you two weren't really dating, and you were just pretending so her ex would leave her alone. So I saw you two interact and it looked realistic. So I-"

She took a gulp of air before continuing her stammering, "I told her it was convincing. I didn't mean it in a bad way, but she clearly was upset-"

I nodded, already having an idea of what went wrong. "Thanks, Georgia."

"I'm sorry, do you want me to-"

I walked around the counter to go find Fox. "No, it's okay I've got it. You didn't do anything wrong."

Looking in the window of her storefront, it was empty. Not even a Link in sight. So I headed around back and reached for my key, but quickly realized I left it in her apartment last night when I slept over. *Fuck*.

"Charlotte, let me in please." I continued knocking on the door for five minutes before giving up. Then I called her. Absolute radio silence.

Fuck. What if she was packing her bags? I was so concerned about taking things slow and not scaring her off that I went *too* slow. And now she probably thought this was all just some game to me. Thinking back to everything we spoke about over the past few hours, I realized I never told her about how I felt. Only how beautiful I thought she was. Fuck.

I paced for a few minutes while I considered my options. So far, the best way to get through to Fox was to be honest with her. But I couldn't exactly explain how I felt when she wouldn't even let me in.

Ultimately, I decided it was best to give her space. She had a habit of running, but I just had to trust that this was something she wanted badly enough to stay. Over the past month she made strides to be successful and happy here in Rosewood. With me.

Returning to the diner, my feet suddenly felt like dead weight. This was going to be the shittiest day ever.

After spending a full shift at the diner trying to distract myself, I went over to Fox's window and played one of the cheesy love songs that we listened to back in high school at practice. Luckily, I kept my playlist all these years, so I had the exact music ready to go.

To my surprise, Fox opened the window and stared at me. She looked very grumpy and her hair fell all around her face in a mess. I couldn't help but worry that she hadn't eaten after leaving her breakfast at my diner.

"What happened to not wanting to ruin the peace?" she called.

I cracked a smile. She was teasing me, and that was a very promising step in the right direction. "Who cares about the peace?"

The street behind us was silent as she waited for me to continue with her elbow resting on the windowsill. "Can you please let me in?"

She disappeared from the window, and my heart sped up at the idea that she was actually going to let me talk to her. The door swung open and I watched her tired eyes stare at my messy clothes from a long day of working in a restaurant.

She invited me in and I followed her quietly up the stairs. "Do you want some tea?"

I was startled at the question. "You drink tea?"

Fox nodded. "Sometimes, when I drink too much coffee."

"Sure, I'll have some tea."

We sat in silence for a little while longer as she poured hot water into a mug and dipped a tea bag in it for me. Being patient would be the death of me, but that was the best route in this situation.

She walked over to the couch with two mugs of tea in her hands and sat down next to me, with plenty of space between us. I took a long slow sip before speaking, "Can we talk about why you're upset now?"

Her head snapped to mine, revealing one of the worst poker faces I had ever seen. "I'm not upset."

I sighed, deciding I would have to do the heavy lifting to steer this conversation in the right direction. Setting my mug down, I held eye contact with Fox. "Georgia told me she mentioned something about us being good at pretending. And then you ran out of the diner and left your pancakes."

It was her turn to set her mug down. "Right, she just put things into perspective. Like a snap back to reality."

"Sweetheart, please tell me you know this isn't pretend," I reasoned. Surely she had to know.

"Well obviously we weren't pretending to fuck each other, but we are friends, and that's it. We took care of my ex, so we have no reason to tell anyone we're anything more."

My heart slowly sunk into my stomach. Some people are afraid of heights, but I say slowly drowning is one of the worst ways to die. At least if you're falling, it's over quickly.

"You just want to be friends," I mimicked with my voice sounding unrecognizable even to me. Then my head hung low. "I knew we shouldn't have gone any further this morning. You were still processing your emotions, I am so sorry."

Fox reached over to grab my hand that was resting on the couch. "We should have, we both wanted that right?"

She waited for me to pick my head up and nod before continuing. "I don't regret this morning at all, and you shouldn't either. But I can't do this full blown relationship thing. I'm not even sure I know how to anymore, and you deserve better than that."

Meeting her eyes, I blew out a long breath. "It would be so easy. You and me, Fox. We could take care of each other, and make each other happy. Wouldn't that be nice?"

Her eyes avoided mine as she looked at the ground. "It's never easy or nice." Retracting her hand away from mine, she met my eyes again. "We can be friends still, with-" She coughed. "Benefits, if that's something you want."

I couldn't stop the laugh from bursting out of me. A long beat of silence fell between us as I processed. "No, I don't want to be friends with benefits, Charlotte." She cringed at the use of her full name.

My pained smile turned to her as I emphasized, "I want *you*. All of your shitty luck, and insistent teasing. Your beautiful brain that manages to work at twice the speed mine does, and this pretty face of yours." My finger slid along her cheek before I moved my hand away.

"All or nothing. So you take your space. I'll be here waiting for you when you're ready, and we can be friends until then, because there is no way I'm staying away from you, Fox."

She cleared her throat and sat rigidly on the edge of the couch as I sprung up from it. "How long are you willing to wait? I have no idea how long it will take until I feel ready, if ever."

"However long you need." I spun around to face the dark window outside. "Have you eaten dinner yet?"

In the reflection of the glass, I saw her shake her head behind me. Telling her I'd be back, I raced downstairs to grab a box of crispy chicken tenders and fries that I made just the way she liked it. Heading back, I stopped at her door when I realized it locked behind me.

I knocked and she opened it for me. "Leftovers," I explained as I handed her the food.

We stared at each other for too long before she thanked me

and we said our goodbyes. And then I was off to have the worst night's sleep of my damn life.

24

Charlotte

Three days after my total fuck up with Reid, and it was the night before opening day. I had barely slept since then, and the only time I was able to sleep was on that shitty couch, so my back was royally fucked. As I tossed and turned for the twentieth time that night, Link rested his paw over my stomach to stop me from moving again. Even he was fed up with me.

We settled down and I tried to focus on breathing to relieve my anxiety. Tomorrow was the big day and I was not going to mess it up. No matter what happened. I hadn't hired any employees because I had no clue how busy it would be, and Evangeline ran her shop on her own most of the time when I was around.

There was no need to stress. Reid showed up the other day to help me put away my food truck and he even organized my walk-in cooler for me. If no one else showed, at least I knew for sure Reid would.

The thought of him sent my mind down another anxiety-riddled path while I worried over how long he would actually wait. How long would it take before he got bitter over my inability to function properly? Never in my life had I felt more broken than when Nicholas Reid said he wanted me.

Lasting until three AM, I got out of bed and headed downstairs in my pajamas to straighten up the cafe. It was already set up perfectly. Not a book was out of place after I spent the last couple of days talking to Dyl over the phone while I fiddled with every single object in the store.

After refolding the same stack of Brewing Pages t-shirts three times, I decided I needed a latte if I wasn't getting any sleep. I limited myself to only two shots of espresso, otherwise the likelihood of having a panic attack skyrocketed. And I had no time for that today. Feeling sorry for myself, I added one sugar to it and sat at one of the tables and drank my latte in silence.

Would Reid show? Of course he would. In all of the time I knew him, he never broke a promise with me. And he made it abundantly clear he was going to stick around even if I wasn't giving him exactly what he wanted.

My mind wasn't listening to logic this morning as it began replaying my usual daydream of me sitting in the shop alone all day and awkwardly waving at people passing by. My stomach felt queasy until I watched Link finally mosey downstairs, and set himself up on his bed next to the windowsill between two of the bookshelves.

A smile took over my face as I watched him sleep while finishing the rest of my latte. Then a figure outside made me flinch and stand up quickly, but when I stared for a little longer I realized it was a small woman standing outside. Setting my latte down, I checked the time to see it was six thirty. The sun was just starting to peek out above the horizon.

Walking over to the door, I cracked it open to apologize and tell her we didn't open until seven. She gave me a huge smile for so early in the morning, "Oh I know, we're just going to wait in line, honey. How exciting! Opening day!"

I looked behind her to see a couple other women walking up from their cars. Then I turned back to her, a smile growing on my own face. "Oh, thank you! Well I will get back to work then, and see you soon."

Going to the back to bring a few more gallons of milk up front, I released a watery laugh while happy tears welled up in the corners of my eyes. Letting out a dorky little jump for joy, I continued on with the milk and set them up front before continuing to check that everything was good to go.

Five minutes before open, I started brewing pots of coffee so it was nice and fresh for everyone. A knock sounded at my back door, and I had a feeling I knew who it was. Checking through my peephole first, I confirmed my suspicions before letting Reid inside.

His smile was gorgeous. "Holy shit. You have a line."

"I have a line!" We took a second to celebrate and he spun me around in a circle before setting me down again.

"Let me help. I can pour coffee, so just point and tell me what to do." I nodded. During my years working at the cafe with Evangeline, I couldn't remember a time when so many people were in the store at once. "Oh, and I brought you some muffins in case you get hungry."

He lifted up a paper bag and set it on one of my tables. "Thank you, Reid." My eyes were still shining with tears, I truly was so grateful for him.

"Anytime, Fox."

190

For the very first time, I turned the sign from closed to open on the front door, swinging it wide and kicking the door stopper to let everyone come in. People moseyed around bookshelves while others beelined to the register to wait for coffee.

Reid was very helpful with pouring coffee for me, while I took orders and cashed people out. When the first latte was ordered, he looked at me helplessly until I walked over and helped him out. Laughing under my breath I asked, "You don't know how to make your own drink of choice?"

He hovered over my shoulder as I worked. "No, we don't have one of these fancy machines in my shop."

The first fifteen minutes was over and the people in line were satisfied with their drinks while they either left to start their day or looked around the store. The three women sat at a table while drinking their coffee and commenting on how different the place looked.

I turned to Reid, "Okay, thank you for your help. Now get back to your diner please."

Putting a hand on his lower back I pretended to push him, but he didn't move. "Are you sure?"

My smile must have reassured him, because it made his concerned look fall into a happy one. "I'm sure, now shoo."

After escorting him to the back door, I returned and offered the three women free t-shirts since they were my very first customers. They were elated and picked out their preferred colors and sizes when a new customer walked through the front door.

Reid walked up to the register without sparing me a second glance. I took a minute to stare and smile at the curls poking out of his hat on the back of his head. Walking around the counter, I stood across from him.

"How can I help you, sir?"

He tried to keep his poker face, but failed horribly. "I'd like my usual, please."

As he took out his wallet, I made sure not to ring anything in so he couldn't pay. Turning my back to him, I began making his drink until I heard a beep over the loud sound of milk steaming.

"*Reid*!" I gasped.

He smiled and walked back around to the customer side of the counter. "You paid in my diner, so now we're even."

"I thought we were even after you fixed my *car*?" I ground out.

He said nothing else as he waited patiently for me to finish and hand him his latte. Even though he had his own business to run, he stuck around for a long time after that. An hour later Reid was at the counter asking me for book recommendations.

"Volleyball for dummies is a great read. Seems like something that could be relevant to you."

He raised an eyebrow and sipped at his latte before muttering, "Or the both of us."

Fully prepared to tell him to get back to his diner, I turned, but got distracted when I saw another familiar face walk in. My therapist. He casually walked up to the counter and ordered a coffee.

I awkwardly agreed and shuffled on my feet as he paid. What's the proper etiquette in that situation? Do I make a joke about how we both offer life changing services? Or say hello doc? Reid standing at the end of the counter staring at me was no help.

In the end, I decided to just play dumb and told him to have a good rest of his day as he walked out. The doctor made no hints that he knew me personally or had ever met me in his entire life. I was a little offended.

"Did you know that guy?" Reid asked.

"Why?"

"You looked like you saw a ghost when he walked in."

I sighed. If I wanted Reid, I needed to continue to make strides in the right direction. He helped me all morning, the least I could do was share a little information. "He's my therapist."

He paused. "You have a therapist?" I nodded. "That's great, Fox. I didn't know, that's really great."

When I looked up again he had a huge smile. "Maybe I should get a therapist too. It's not a bad idea." My eyebrows raised and I processed the fact that he wasn't teasing me or being awkward at all. Huh.

25

Nick

Fox's opening day went better than she could have imagined and I was so damn proud of her. I stayed for the first couple of hours to make sure she was okay, and made sure to check in on her every hour or so after that. After taking out her trash around lunch, she gave me a playful smile.

"I'm never going to be able to pay you back for all of this free labor you're giving me."

Paying attention to my hands so I didn't touch her again without meaning to, I kept them firmly at my sides. One of her locks of hair was falling in her face and I was dying to tuck it behind her ear for her. "Don't worry about it, Fox."

Brewing Pages closed at six PM, so when she was finished, I headed over to her back door. She opened after the first couple of knocks with a huge smile on her face.

"How does it feel?"

"Amazing, I can't believe I did it. I survived! And so many people showed up. Lots of them even said they would be back tomorrow." She moved back to let me in when she saw a box in my hands. "What's this?"

"Cinnamon roll french toast. I figured we could try it together for the first time." That was a little bit of a fib. I made about ten batches of different cinnamon roll french toast recipes, but this one looked like it was going to finally live up to my standards.

She looked away from the box and back to my face. "You're serious?"

I nodded and led her to one of her cafe tables. Pulling out forks for each of us, I handed her one and sat down to open up the box. "Holy shit, it smells amazing."

Fox took the first bite and I watched for her reaction. Her face somehow lit up even more, and she nodded while she chewed. The second she swallowed she declared, "Ten stars. Absolutely ten stars."

I dove in to try it out for myself and see if I agreed. My eyebrows raised too as I ate my first bite. The berry compote I put on top really made the dish, the acidity cut through all of the sugar. And the cinnamon roll 'bread' wasn't too thick, it practically melted in my mouth.

"It is so damn good, Reid. Seriously, you're some kind of wizard."

We finished off the dessert in record time while commenting on different things we liked about it. Fox made me promise to make it for her at least once a month. I agreed, but a sad pang hit my chest.

It was time to go, because we were just friends. For now. I got up to leave and congratulated her one last time before walking out the door. She stopped me with a hand on my wrist.

"Thank you so much for all you did today, Reid. It meant a lot to me." And then she pushed to her tiptoes and gave me a sweet kiss on the cheek.

That was definitely progress.

* * *

A few days later and I was anxiously awaiting for Lane Gilbert's arrival. She was due today but didn't give me a set time for when she would show. I was excited to see what she would order, and I was absolutely going to recommend she try Fox's french toast afterward.

She showed up just as dinner rush began, and I let my server know to be on his best behavior. I walked around and introduced myself. She had an air of confidence, but nothing was going to rattle my nerves. Returning to the kitchen, I waited for her order to come in.

Grilled cheese. The food critic ordered a damn grilled cheese. "Paul, tell me what the woman said exactly."

"She said she wants a grilled cheese, and to tell the chef to have fun with it." What the fuck?

Fine, if she wanted a grilled cheese, it was going to be the best sandwich she had ever had in her life. I got to work and brainstormed a few ideas while chopping up tomatoes. Twenty minutes later, I personally served the dish to her and described the tomato and beef bacon filled grilled cheese made with white cheddar and mozzarella.

I sat down in the back while I waited for the results. I was unsure if she would even tell me what she thought today, or if I would have to wait until her review was posted online. My server walked up and I fixed him with my total attention.

"Hey, Charlotte is here. Thought you might want to know." I nodded and hopped up to go greet her.

Walking over to the most beautiful woman in the world, I couldn't help but peek out of the corner of my eye to see if Lane was enjoying the food. She finished half of the sandwich already, so that seemed promising.

"Hey, Fox." She gave me a small smile. "I have some cinnamon roll french toast, if you want it today?"

Her eyes brightened as she nodded. "Can I have a burger first though? I'm starved."

"Of course, let me go tell Jace." I wrote down her order and put the ticket on the board for Jace before returning to stand in front of Fox.

Now Lane was pulling apart the second half of the sandwich to pick at each individual ingredient with her fork. Who the fuck eats a grilled cheese like that?

"Reid?" My attention was drawn back to Fox. "Who is that you keep staring at?"

I shushed her, so she would keep her voice down. "She's a food critic. I invited her here to try out the diner. This has to go well, people follow her food blog like it's gospel."

"She'll love it. I'm the toughest food critic, remember? And I gave you ten stars, so she'll be blown away by your food."

"She ordered a grilled cheese," I said mindlessly.

Fox was quiet for a bit before continuing, "Even your grilled cheeses are great."

I fixed her with a teasing smile. "You're awfully sweet lately, Fox."

"Whatever," she muttered. Her lips pulled up at the corners and she looked down. Picking up her phone from the counter, she played with it until her food arrived.

I was enthralled as Lane picked up her sandwich and put it back together to finish the entire thing. She wrote down notes on her pad of paper the entire time Fox ate. My server checked on her a few times, but she insisted she needed to be left alone.

"Well I've got to get back. I have books to restock, and a bank run to make," Fox said.

I nodded to her. "Okay, good luck."

"Let me know how this goes, I've had quite the show with dinner today." Her playful smile caused my eyes to roll like a knee jerk reaction.

"See you tomorrow, Fox."

26

Charlotte

The high of opening the store slowly faded as I found myself wanting to talk Reid's ear off about it every day. Sure, we still saw each other, but I found myself wishing it was more than it was. But that was something I talked about with my therapist, and we both agreed it was best to stick to my boundaries until I was absolutely certain I wanted more with Reid.

No matter how hard that was.

I was restocking my self-help section of the store when Georgia walked in. Link popped his head up as if he was silently greeting her before going back to his nap.

"Hey," she sounded awkward and I barely heard her over a couple that was chatting at one of the cafe tables.

We hadn't seen each other since I ran out of Reid's that morning, she probably thought I was completely insane now. "Hey, I am so sorry about the other day."

She raised her hand to stop me. "No, I'm sorry. I should have kept my big mouth shut, and I promise I was not trying to upset you."

"I know, and you didn't. I was just really in my head and you said something that resonated with me."

Georgia nodded and stepped closer. "So, we're still friends?"

Smiling at the innocent question, I nodded. "Of course." I turned to gesture at the books. "Now do you want the ultimate grand tour?"

She nodded excitedly and waited for me to set down the box I was working on. I walked her down each aisle and pointed at the different sections, noting some of the books I had special editions of. As we walked she picked out books that interested her, and by the time we were finished, our arms were full of books she wanted to buy.

"Ruth is going to absolutely adore Percy Jackson. It might be a little bit too much for her age, but I think if we read it together she'll enjoy it," Georgia said.

We put the books on the counter and I got a couple of bags for her. "I'm sure she will, it's an absolute classic. Do you want a coffee too?"

"Yes, please!" She finished telling me her coffee order and I started making her latte while she paid. "So, would you want to go out to dinner tonight with me and Reese? Are you busy?"

I turned around to place the cup in front of her. "That sounds so nice. I honestly need to get out of this place and do anything other than work for a little while."

Georgia laughed and grabbed her bags while I continued, "I close at six, so I can be free at six thirty?"

"I'll come and pick you up, then." She gave me one last shy smile before waving and struggling to carry two bags and her latte all at the same time.

Dressed in a flowy cherry red dress and my favorite strappy sandals, I walked next to Reese and Georgia to the taco place that we were eating at tonight. They insisted Link come along too since the place has an outside patio, so he was happily trotting alongside us.

Our food was delivered at record speed while we sipped on margaritas and Link lazily laid next to me with his head resting on top of my foot. My cheeks hurt a little from laughing and I was grateful to have friends in my town to hang out with. Although, I did wish Dyl could be there too.

Reese was off into a story about how one of her freshmen got pregnant and was planning on bringing the baby to school to finish her degree after it was born. "Her parents were talking as if it was a crazy idea, but I am so proud of her for planning to still get an education."

Her hand stirred the margarita sitting in front of her while she continued, "I can't imagine raising a baby under such stressful circumstances, though. Hopefully she has the support she needs."

Georgia and I nodded as the laughter quickly died. Reese turned to Georgia. "So, have you told Charlotte the exciting news yet? Or is it a secret?"

Georgia's shy smile turned to me. "It's really not that big of a deal, but I'm writing my own book. It's going to be a fictional book for kids a little bit older than Ruth's age."

My eyebrows raised. "That's so exciting! I thought you already published a book though?"

"Ah, that one I was ghostwriting for someone else. But this one will have my name on it and everything." Her proud smile was endearing.

"That is so great, I can't wait to stock it on my shelves." The three of us shared a cheesy moment where we all smiled at each other before continuing to eat.

Georgia piped up again after a minute, "We should cheers to all of our success. Charlotte opened her shop, Reese is molding the minds of the youth, and I'm writing a book!"

We all shared a look before raising our glasses. Confidently I spoke, "To us."

They repeated my words and we all clinked glasses before taking a drink. A minute later I caught Reese and Georgia sharing a strange look. It occurred to me that I should probably explain what happened the other day with Reid.

Before I could think of how to start that conversation, Georgia did it for me. "So, I might have told Reese about what happened the other day at the diner."

The two looked at me guilt-ridden. I laughed, "That's okay. I was just thinking of how to explain that."

Reese asked, "What's going on with you two?"

"Well, we're just friends. But we sort of slipped into more than friends territory for a bit, so I freaked out. And now we're strictly friends again."

They shared an incredibly confused look. "Don't you like him? He is clearly embarrassingly in love with you."

Choking at Reese's bold claim, I set down my glass. Choosing my words carefully was hard, because I wanted to be open and honest, but it felt weird to talk about something so personal with anyone other than Reid or Dyl.

"I do like him. A lot. But after everything with my ex, I'm not sure I'm ready for a relationship. And that's exactly what Reid wants."

Georgia nodded. "That makes sense. It's a hard situation, I heard about how he tried to break in."

"Yeah, thank God Nick was there."

Reese broke her silence again to add, "It seems like you care about him a lot too. I'm assuming you two talked about this already?"

"We did, he says he'll wait for me to be ready. But I have no idea how long that will take."

Georgia snickered a little. "Reid's can be patient as hell, if Ash is any testament to that. I'm sure he'll wait as long as you need."

The words reassured me and I sat back in my seat with a stomach full of delicious tacos. As we all finished our food we asked for the check, paid, and returned to the car. I slipped into the back with Link while the two other women sat up front.

Reese turned to look at us with an overdramatic frown. "I don't want this to be over."

I laughed and offered, "We can all go back to mine if you want. I don't have any other plans tonight."

We ended up stopping at a liquor store to buy a bottle of wine and went up to my loft to drink out of oversized glasses and watch cheesy rom coms. It was late at night when we finished the last movie and both Reese and Georgia were tipsy, so I let them pass out on my couch. Thankfully it was big enough for two people.

I crawled into bed with Link around two am and smiled into his fur happily as he snuggled into me. Falling into a comfortable sleep was easy. Until my morning alarm woke us all up with its insistent beeping.

Hearing a groan from the couch, I explained, "I have to go

open the cafe."

Throwing the blanket off of me, I squinted my eyes while I tried to find a bottle of water laying around somewhere. My head was pounding, we totally overdid it last night. Reese sat up with a huff, "Why the hell would you *choose* to wake up so early?"

I chuckled, but quickly stopped when the action made another lightning bolt of pain go through my head. "Don't you have to be at the school in a few hours anyway?"

"Shit." Georgia popped up her head a couple of minutes later as I was exiting the bathroom and Reese was tugging on her shoes. "Can I use your bathroom?"

"Go for it, I'll be downstairs if you two need anything. Feel free to help yourselves to whatever you need." I opened the door. "Except my toothbrush."

I prepared the cafe for a brand new day and started brewing coffee a few minutes before seven. Right as I was preparing to unlock the front door, Reese and Georgia popped into view looking as hungover as ever. I laughed and pointed at two to-go cups of coffee for them to drink.

Reese came over to hug me before leaving. "If you ever want part time workers so you don't have to go through this hell of a wake up call everyday, let me know. I'm sure some of my students would love to work here."

I chuckled and said my goodbyes to both of them before they snuck out the back door and went home. Nursing my own headache with some mint tea and ibuprofen, I quickly went upstairs to see if I had anything for breakfast.

* * *

The day was long and slow in between customers. Even after opening day, we were as busy as I had ever seen the cafe in the days of Evangeline. I suspected I wasn't the only one who had been hoping for a bookstore in Rosewood.

Reid hadn't made any appearances all day. Usually he came in for a coffee at least once a day, but today so far he was a no show. I wondered if he was busy with something important. Suddenly insecure about the status of our relationship, my mind wandered off to other things that he could be doing than spending time with me.

Right before close, my mind became totally irrational after daydreaming for the last two hours about Reid not wanting to be with me anymore. I walked up to one of my chairs and 'accidentally' pushed it over to slam onto the floor.

Link flinched and I instantly felt regretful. "Sorry buddy, I wasn't trying to scare you."

Inspecting the chair, I found it totally intact. Not even a dent or splintering of wood. I muttered curse words under my breath.

Leaning over, I found a screw and quickly went to go find my screw driver. Loosening the screw, I pulled it out and stuffed it in my pocket. The chair leg fell off after I set the chair back on the ground and the leg loudly slammed to the floor.

I looked to Link who was now my accomplice. "Oh no, the chair broke. What a shame." And then I walked over to Reid's diner.

27

Nick

The diner had been unusually busy all day. So busy that I didn't have time to sneak over to Fox's cafe this morning which made me a little grumpier than usual. I was beginning to think I not only had an addiction to her, but her coffee as well.

I was handing out plates to a couple when I saw her walk through the door. She looked absolutely gorgeous today in a sweater and those tight blue jeans that showed off her ass. As the weather was cooling off, I found myself appreciating a new side of her wardrobe that I hadn't seen before.

She walked straight up to me. "Here for dinner?"

"No, I actually was going to ask if you have a tool box I can borrow," she stated. Her hands slid into the back pockets of her jeans as she confidently stood in the middle of my diner.

"What the hell do you need a toolbox for?" I started walking to the back while she trailed behind me.

She greeted Jace as we passed him and started explaining, "Well one of my-"

Grabbing my toolbox, I pushed open my back door and held it for her. "Just show me and I'll fix it for you."

Her eyes rolled, but her lips held a very satisfied smile. Inside her cafe, she led me to a table that had a broken leg laying on the ground next to it. Link stood up and trotted over to me to say hello.

I pet his head and let him lick my fingers before turning to the task at hand. Sitting on the ground, I got to work while Fox sat on the chair next to me and watched.

"How was your day?" she asked.

My eyes flicked to hers for a second before continuing to look for the right screw that would fit the chair. "It was good, very busy. Lane put up her review and apparently it was good because we've had a flood of people today."

"Really? That's amazing, I want to read it." I chuckled and continued searching.

"Let me know what she says because I haven't gotten a chance to yet."

"You're that busy? Well here, let me fix this then," She sat on the ground next to me and started reaching for my toolbox.

I put my hand on hers to stop her. "Why don't you just read it out loud so we can read it together? And I'll do this?"

Fox found the blog post and read aloud the glowing review. I heard the smile in her voice when she got to the part about how Lane adored the 'revolutionary' cinnamon roll french toast. When she finished, she shuffled toward me to wrap her arms around my shoulders.

"I am so proud of you. This is amazing, Reid!" My smile from ear to ear wasn't just from the good review.

"Thanks, I couldn't have done it without you." She scoffed and playfully pushed my shoulder.

We sat in happy silence while I found the screw and set the chair on its side to reattach the chair leg. Fox's knee bumped into mine as she handed me the leg.

A long pause before she shocked me. "Do you ever think about your mom?" My hands froze and I blinked before turning to her. She cringed, "Sorry, I ruined the moment."

"No, I was just surprised. What got you thinking about that?"

"I've been thinking about mine a little lately and wondered if you ever think about yours. She was sort of absent in high school, and now you never mention her so-"

"Yeah, after we graduated and Ash went pro, she barely reaches out. Last I heard, she was on some great road trip on the west coast. But that was years ago." The screwdriver was held a little more firmly in my hand now.

"Does that bother you?" Her voice was quiet but interested.

"Not anymore. It used to a little, but I had Ash, so it didn't matter too much. It's not like she was mom of the year before she dropped contact." I sighed and then something else popped into my brain. "It bothered Ash a lot more when Ruthie was born. I hated her a little, too. Because how could she not want to meet her own grandchild, and the coolest kid on the planet."

Fox nodded silently and I looked up to see a tear streaming down her face. I used my thumb to rub it off. She chuckled softly, "Sorry, that just makes me hate her a little too. I can't imagine anyone not wanting you in their life. Or Ruth."

"Me either." Now for the question I had been wanting to ask for years. "What happened with your mom? You lived with her before you came to Rosewood, right?"

She wiped another stray tear. "Sort of a similar situation. Ever since I was old enough to talk she would disappear sometimes. I had a job at twelve to try to pay the bills, but when I was thirteen we got evicted and she was nowhere to be found."

"I didn't want to go into foster care, so I hopped on a bus and found the only other family I knew of. Evangeline." I pulled her into a hug and she rested her head on my shoulder for a bit.

After a minute she pushed me back gently and laughed. "Sorry, I don't know where that came from."

"Is this the sort of thing you talk about in therapy?"

"Yeah, actually it is." She laughed again and used the sleeve of her shirt to wipe her face. "It feels weird to talk about, but I'm glad I know more about you now."

"Yeah, me too Fox."

I turned back to the chair and finished fixing it while we sat in silence. When I was done we stood and she thanked me again. Unable to help myself, I tucked that same stubborn piece of hair behind her ear before telling her goodnight.

She looked into my eyes before grabbing my hand to give it a quick squeeze. "Goodnight, Reid."

* * *

A few days later Fox came into my diner again. Every day lately, it seemed she was surprising me in new ways. She was opening up more, and I was so damn happy she felt comfortable doing that with me.

Today she sat down for breakfast while I was also sitting at the bar working on my laptop. Hopping up on the stool next to me, she asked what I was working on.

"New menus, I'm adding some new stuff, so I figured I'd do an overhaul of the whole menu." I slid the laptop over so she could see the document I was working on. "Are you any good at this stuff?"

"Yeah I know a thing or two after designing everything for the bookstore, I can help if you want." She leaned in to get a closer look.

I smiled and tugged at her braid. "Thanks, what do you want for breakfast?"

"Hmm, today I want blueberry pancakes."

"Sounds good."

We ate breakfast together at the bar while she gave me ideas for how to design the menu. She even taught me a little bit about the editing software I was using and shared what she learned about different color associations when she designed her logo.

An hour later she got up to go open her shop. "Good luck, let me know if you have any other questions."

"I will. We're totally even on free labor now by the way." Her eyes rolled and she shot me a smile.

"See you later."

I watched her leave and was hit with guilt. A few days ago I thought of a crazy idea that might help the both of us sleep a little easier at night. And I hoped to God she wouldn't hate me for it.

That night after I closed, I sat and waited a long while until a familiar shadow in the window caught my eye.

28

Charlotte

I anxiously paced around my apartment and checked the clock for the millionth time that morning. Today was the first adoption event I was taking Link to, and I was so damn nervous. He was being a good boy though, as he watched me walk around frantically.

We made it to the car and sat for a moment while I collected myself. His vet told me about this event, and said it would be a great opportunity for finding Link a permanent home. Honestly, until she mentioned it I was operating under the idea that he was just mine now.

He fit in so well with my life, we loved our early morning walks and the customers adored getting to say hi to him as much as he enjoyed the extra attention. For fuck's sake, I created a spot next to the window just for him to hang out in.

The hard part was that Link wasn't my dog, this was just a temporary situation. He needed a proper home with a family that cared about him. Sure, I did okay after we got to know each other, but if there was a home out there with people that could take better care of him than I could, he totally deserved that.

Clicking my seatbelt, I gave him a scratch behind his ears and pulled his muzzle close to give him a quick kiss. He licked my ear in response and I shoved my emotions deep down in my soul.

We pulled up before the start time of the event, but people were already walking about. The parking lot was busy and we got out to people-watch for a bit before slowly wandering around the edge of the huge park. There were blankets spread out everywhere, and little pens where puppies were free to play.

I clipped the 'Looking for a Home' tag to Link's harness and took in a deep breath. We stood there on the edge of the grass, watching the event start up for a long while. Dogs and people greeted each other and happily pranced around the park.

Fuck. Looking down at Link, I snatched the sign off of his harness and walked us back to the car. He hopped in the backseat without me even asking and I leaned down to scratch behind his ear. "Do you wanna come home with me bud?"

He cheekily licked my nose and I took that as a yes. Tears fully streaming down my cheeks, I drove us back home. There was no way in hell Link could be anyone's dog except for mine. How would they know what bones he favors? What if they didn't add a little splash of water to his food how he liked? They might not even scratch behind his ears correctly.

We sat in my car for a minute before I collected myself. He led the way back inside and once I took off his harness and leash he ran for his bed and tucked himself in. I walked up and sat down on the floor in front of him.

"You're going to stay here, okay? Would that make you

happy?" He just stared at me. How the hell do you tell if a dog is happy?

Needing to talk to someone, I called up Dyl. "Hey, Char."

"Hey, do you think I'd make a good parent?"

Dylan took a quick pause. "Holy shit, are you *crying*? Are you pregnant?"

"Hell no, dog parent, I meant. I was supposed to take Link to an adoption event today, but I don't want him to find a new family. He belongs here."

A small laugh sounded through the phone. "Then you keep him, Char."

"It's not that easy, what if he's not happy here? I've never had a dog, what if I'm not doing things that I should be? There are certainly better parents out there for him than me. He deserves to be happy."

She interrupted my rambling. "You talk to me about this dog nearly every single day. You feed him chicken and buy him bones and toys, and he goes practically everywhere you go, right?"

"Well sort of, yes. But I could be doing more."

"Char, that dog loves you. And you love him, right?"

"Yes, I do." My throat tightened again. Never in my entire life had I cried so much as I had in the past month. Emotions were so exhausting.

"Then he's your dog. That's all there is to it. You both make each other happy and better each other's lives. Sure, there may be some famous celebrity out there that could feed him caviar every day and buy a swimming pool for him. But no one else loves that dog as much as you do."

The phone line went silent and I covered my face with my free hand. "Are you crying again?"

I laughed and mumbled through my tears, "Of fucking course I am."

Dylan laughed at me. "The magical effects of therapy everyone! It really has done wonders on you, I can't believe you're not only crying, but talking to me about your *feelings*." The phone line crackled. "I really need to get onboard the second my insurance goes through. These doctors are working miracles out here."

"Shut up," I whispered with a smile on my face.

"I love you, Char."

"I love you too, Dyl."

Link rested his head against my hand. "Now go cuddle your dog! And tell him hello for me."

Hanging up the phone, I did just that. Link and I spent the day together going on another long walk and hanging out in my apartment upstairs. I taught him some new tricks and we even went to a pet store to buy him a big new bone and a tag for his collar with my information in case he got lost again. Which I totally expected would happen.

At night, I cooked us up some bland grilled chicken with no seasoning so I could share with Link. We enjoyed our dinner and watched a movie together on the couch. As it got later into the night, I couldn't help but feel like something was missing. My heart was much fuller than it had ever been, but there was still one final piece gone.

I imagined what it would be like to have Reid here now. I hadn't seen him all day. Something about what Dylan said struck a chord in me, no one loves Link more than I do. And I severely doubted anyone could love Reid more than I did, except for maybe Ruth.

Was that really all there was to it? I felt more ready for a relationship than I ever had before, but nothing really changed. Had it? Looking out the window, I felt a sudden flash of determination and put on slippers to go head outside. It was only ten fifteen, so he was probably still closing up the diner.

I walked around front to see if I could spot him through the window. He wasn't behind the counter, but the light was still on so I opened the door to walk in. Thankfully, it was still unlocked and out of the corner of my eye I saw him sitting at a table.

Fully turning toward him, the smile on my face washed into horror as I took in who was sitting across from him. Reid stood up and spoke quietly, "Charlotte."

But at that point my ears had already started ringing. Spinning on my feet, I turned right back to where I came from. Link greeted me at the door and I made sure to lock it behind me before running up to my apartment and shutting us both inside.

Motherfucker.

29

Nick

Shit.

This was not the way I intended this to go. I finished up my conversation with Fox's ex and threw the check at him. "You stay the fuck away from her."

"Got it, this was all I wanted. You won't be hearing from me again." He stood up from the chair to grab the check before sliding it in his pocket.

I made sure to watch him get in his car and drive off before locking my diner and sprinting to Fox's back door. Both the front and back door were locked so I stood as close to her window as I could before yelling, "Fox! Please let me in."

Nothing. "I need to talk to you-"

From behind me another window opened in a building close to us. "Stop that racket, some of us are trying to sleep!"

"Sorry! I'll just be a minute." I said to the old woman with her head shoved out of her window. Then I turned back to Fox's building. "Please, there is an explanation. Just let me in and we can talk. Please don't run, I'll follow you anywhere you want me to. But I need to talk to you first."

My yelling probably woke up the whole neighborhood, but the only response I got was a shrill 'shut up' from the woman across the alley. Sighing, I knew that meant Fox wasn't going to talk to me tonight.

So I slid against her door until I was sitting on the concrete in front of it. There was no chance I would break her trust like that asshole and try to force my way inside. All night I sat there on that concrete, leaning against her door.

* * *

I felt something push into my back and jumped awake. The door behind me was trying to open and sunlight assaulted my eyes. Through the door, I heard mumbling so I scooted out of the way and it flew open.

"What the fuck-" Charlotte's voice was high pitched as she shrieked. "Reid! What the hell are you doing?"

Blinking, I stood up to start the speech that I planned out in my head before falling asleep. "Listen, it wasn't what it looked like. I was trying to give you peace of mind-"

"Have you been out here all night?"

I nodded and tried to pick up where I left off, but she dropped the trash bag in her hands and put herself under one of my arms. We walked like that with me leaning on her up the stairs and into her apartment. Still a little disarmed by the wakeup call, I struggled to string together words that I needed to say.

"Sit." She pointed to her couch and then went to grab something as I sunk into it. The cushions were so god damn cushiony.

A glass of water was shoved into my hand and I drank half of it in one go. She took it from me and set it down on the table. Realizing this was the moment I was waiting for, I started again, "I invited him to my diner to talk out a solution-"

She interrupted me yet again. "You were seriously out there all night to say this to me?"

"Yes, now will you please-"

"No, lay down. You're insane, Reid. Is your diner covered for today?"

I nodded. "It's Monday, right? Jace is opening, so they don't need me."

"Okay, well lay down please and get some sleep. I'll take care of everything." The offer sounded so damn nice. I was going to disagree again until she pushed me on my back so I was laying down. She returned with a pillow to put under my head and covered me up with a blanket.

I was in dreamland for who knows how long. It certainly wasn't the morning anymore, because the hot sun was in full force and the noise of a busy street was audible from outside. To my left, I found Fox setting out a bowl of food.

"Perfect timing, you should eat," she said. "I'm no chef, and I have no food, so it's just cereal. I hope that's okay."

Slowly sitting up, I took in my surroundings a little more. "I told Jace you wouldn't be coming in today. He said they've got the diner covered, so you don't need to worry."

Nodding, I stared into her pretty green eyes. Her hair was swept off her neck with a clip and the ends of her hair splayed out in a bunch of different directions like a peacock.

"What about Brewing Pages?" I mumbled.

"I kept it open for a few hours, but I decided to close after lunch." I hummed and reached for the cereal bowl to start eating. I was fucking starved.

Charlotte sat down next to me and ate her own bowl. We were silent as I processed everything that happened last night and this morning. She took care of me, which I was eternally grateful for. The things I was planning on saying shouldn't be said when I was practically unconscious from lack of sleep.

We set our bowls down and Fox turned her body to fully face me. "So you wanted to explain what happened last night?"

I turned to face her too and took a deep breath. "Yes, if that's okay."

She nodded, encouraging me to continue. Although she was turned toward me, her body language was closed off and uncomfortable and I absolutely hated it. I needed her to trust me again.

"First off, I was going to tell you. But I wanted to make sure it went well first, so I didn't cause you any more stress."

Her arms crossed in front of her torso. "What is *it*?"

"The deal I made." She was silent, so I continued. "A few nights ago I saw him sitting in a car across from the diner. I went over and told him to fuck off, but obviously that wasn't going to do much."

Her face was incredulous. "And you didn't tell me? Or the police?"

"He technically wasn't breaking your restraining order since he was across the street. And he was in his car, so he would have just driven off." Another pause from her. "So, I had an idea. I found him online and reached out to him to figure out what the fuck it is he wanted."

"The engagement ring. But I pawned it off, it's gone," she argued.

"Well turns out he wanted the money from the engagement

ring. Apparently his company is going bankrupt, I even looked it up online to see if his story checked out and it's true."

Her head tilted in confusion. "So I met with him and gave him money for the ring. That was all it was, no more than a ten minute conversation. And now he's gone for good."

She leveled me with a stare and kept her arms crossed. "You should have told me."

"I realize that now, and I'm sorry. But I didn't want you to feel unsafe, especially because he was waiting in front of your shop."

She huffed. "I realize I've been slightly more in tune with my emotions lately, but that does not mean you get to decide what I can handle."

Her tone felt like a slap to the face. She was absolutely damn right, but my stubborn ass just wanted to keep her safe. "You're right."

"How much did you pay him?"

"Ten thousand." Her eyes bugged out of her head. Uncrossing her arms, she leaned in close.

"You gave him ten *thousand* dollars?"

I nodded. "That was his number, so I paid it."

Pinching the bridge of her nose with her fingers, she hung her head for a long moment. "I'm paying you back."

"No, this was my decision and-"

"You've made enough decisions, Reid. I'm paying you for this. That is the only way I am accepting this crazy fucking thing you did."

I thought for a long moment. Did that mean she would forgive me? Accepting was a little bit different than forgiving. "Okay."

She glared at me. "Okay?" I nodded in confirmation.

"I'm not sure how to feel," she confessed.

"That's probably normal, Fox. You take all the time you need to process-"

She cut me off and quickly snapped, "Do you know why I was going over to your diner late at night?"

My head shook. That was something I hadn't even considered yet. She continued to shock me with her words. "There was a lot of stuff I wanted to say, and now I don't remember any of it. I decided to adopt Link and Dyl said something about-"

She huffed and pulled at her hair out of frustration. Then her eyes met mine and she looked through my damn soul. "I love you. That's basically what I wanted to say."

My heart went on a fucking rollercoaster ride. It contracted at the thought of Fox loving me too, and then it sunk deep into my chest when I realized I already fucked it up. But she loved me. Charlotte Fox loved me.

Her body language now read as vulnerable while she waited for my response. "I love you, Fox. More than anything."

She let out a breath I didn't realize she was holding. Then she inspected her hands and nodded to herself. I spoke again, "Do you think you can forgive me?"

"I already have. Which is so fucking dumb-" I launched across the couch to pull her into a hug. She laughed at me and wrapped her arms around my waist. "I'm still mad at you."

I pulled back with a huge smile on my face. "I'll make it up to you, I promise."

"You're taking out my trash for an entire year. Coffee grounds are heavy."

"Make it fifty years and I'm game." She rolled her eyes at my offer and pulled me into another hug. "I love you."

Our gazes met again and our noses touched. "I love you," she whispered. With her eyes closed she muttered, "Please don't do anything totally fucking moronic like that again. I felt like I was having a heart attack."

"I promise I won't," I spoke my promise into her ear and I fucking meant it.

30

Charlotte

Nicholas Reid was so fucking mine. He *loved* me. Never in my life had someone said that to me and I believed they actually meant it. Except for maybe Evangeline, that woman loved everyone.

Sitting in his lap now, I admired his pretty eyelashes and dorky lovesick smile. His eyes held cartoon hearts in them as he looked up at me. "We are so embarrassing," I said through my smile.

"Not at all, Fox. This is what I've wanted this entire time, you're the one that's just now catching up." Yeah, right.

His nose nudged mine and I accepted his kiss happily. We made out on the couch with his hands resting on the back of my neck and my waist. Mine were firmly planted on his shoulders as I balanced myself on top of him.

He pulled back and nipped at my cheek, "Do you need food? Cereal is not a meal."

I sighed at his need to constantly care for me, but it was quite a nice feeling. "No, I'm not hungry right now."

Accepting my answer, he leaned in for another kiss. This time I pulled back, "Are you hungry?"

He laughed at my worrying. "Only for you." My eyes rolled obnoxiously at the cheesy line and he chuckled again at my reaction. "Don't worry, Fox. You'll get used to it."

"I have a feeling you're right." Hand behind my neck, he pulled my head forward again until we were locked in another kiss. I started subtly grinding on him when I felt his hard on pressing into my jeans.

Groaning, he spoke right into my ear and I instantly flushed in excitement. "Are you sure about this? We don't have to, right this second."

"I would really prefer if we did," I breathlessly responded.

Leaning back on his lap, I grabbed the hem of my long sleeved top and pulled it over my head to reveal my lacy blue bralette. "Fuck." His hands immediately went to my tits and squeezed.

I laughed at his behavior and he gripped my chin to pull me into another kiss. Suddenly distracted, I melted into the kiss again and firmly pushed my body as close to his as I could. His hands wrapped around my back to unclasp the lacy material.

"You're going to kill me one day, Fox. You and your body and your smart mouth will be the death of me."

Once it was unclasped he pulled back a little to rip it off and toss it to the side. His eyes appreciated my body before his hands found my tits and did their own form of appreciation. He squeezed, pulled, and pinched at me until I was far too impatient for him to be fully clothed.

I tugged at his black t-shirt. "I want this off now."

He obliged and reached behind his neck to pull it up and over his head. Watching his muscles move with him as he threw it to the ground, I was fully mesmerized. A playful smile was on his lips when he tipped my chin up again and his lips met mine.

"Better?" I nodded. So much better. My hands felt up his abdomen, they were much less defined than when we were in school, but he was so much bigger now. More manly and less gangly. I was totally missing out all those days since we last did this.

He nipped at my ear and returned his attention to my neck while his hands paved their own path down my body. I whimpered into his hot kisses and I felt his tongue lash out to soothe a spot he nipped a bit too hard. Amused, he pulled back and met my gaze. "Your neck is really sensitive."

Huffing, I pushed him until his back was pressed to the couch cushions and his body was in full view for me. "Yes, I am well aware, asshole."

A smirk took over his lips and his hands returned to my waist. In a flash, I was moved with my back to the couch and Reid loomed over me. "I want to make you feel so damn good. Do you know how many times I've imagined this since I had you last?"

He started kissing up my neck again and all thoughts left my head. He answered his own question. "Too damn many."

Moving away from me, he reached for his belt and undid it before pulling down his pants. He reached for my own when I started unbuttoning them and pushed my hands away to do it himself. "I'm going to take my time with you, Fox. I want to make you feel as crazy as I do every time I look at you."

He yanked down my pants and underwear and shoved them to the side before doing the same with his own. I took in the sight of him naked and thought about how lucky I was to see this more often.

Sitting back on his knees, he picked up one of my feet to kiss my ankle before placing it over his shoulder. Then he moved until his head was between my thighs and I could feel his hot breath on my cunt.

"Fuck, Reid." I was already arching up into him. He needed to hurry the fuck up.

His thumb lightly brushed my clit as he teased me by dragging it all the way down to my center. "You're so fucking wet, baby."

He gave a quick kiss to my thigh before diving in. I gasped as I felt him lick his way around my cunt messily. This was much different from last time where he was slow and gentle to figure out what I liked. He was being greedy and taking exactly what he wanted from me.

My leg that was hanging over his shoulder bent until it was laying across his back. He groaned into me when he felt my thighs clench and wrapped an arm under one of them to hold it still. My moans pitched an octave when I felt him push a single finger into me and he continued sucking at my clit.

I was falling over the edge before I knew it. He had two fingers pushed into me now and was moving them in a slow rhythm with his tongue before speeding up again. Pulling at his hair, my legs clenched around him again.

"Please, Reid. Fuck, please." Gasping for breath, he didn't stop until I hit my climax. He slowed down as my thighs trembled and I started pushing at his head. When it was clear my orgasm was done he pulled his head up and wiped my wetness with the back of his hand.

He smiled up at me wildly. Catching my breath, I moved my hand from his hair to his shoulder as he climbed up my body and captured me in another kiss. I pushed him away after a minute to breathe.

"You okay?" he asked. I brushed back a piece of his hair that hung in his forehead.

"Mhm, I'm great." Laughing at my dopey smile, he kissed my nose before backing up again.

Wrapping my arms around his neck, he moved his hands under my ass until I was in a sitting position and firmly wrapped around him like a koala. He picked me up and I let my head fall into the crook of his neck while he walked.

"Where are we going?"

He dropped me onto my bed. I opened my eyes again to see his smile. "The first time we fuck properly is going to be a bed. I hope that's okay with you."

My eyebrow quirked and I sat up on my elbows. "We didn't fuck properly last time?"

He rolled his eyes and pulled at one of my toes before leveling me with a sexy stare. "I meant as two people in a committed relationship."

"Oh, relationship sex. Should I give you a star rating, then?"

Collapsing on top of me, he smothered me with his shoulder and I pushed at his heavy frame. "You're going to get it if you don't watch your mouth."

Both of us laughing, he stared into my eyes and pushed hair out of my face to get a good look at me. His words were soft and meant for me and me alone. "You really are so beautiful."

I kissed his hand and quietly added, "So are you." He chuckled, but I fully meant it.

He met me with another mind melting kiss and slowly pushed inside of me. We both groaned at the sudden feeling and I clenched down on his dick. Then he began his slow and thorough thrusts before making eye contact with me while he fucked me.

The sex was slow and sweet, just like Reid. I lost my mind in pleasure and let him take control as he made love to me while murmuring all the things that we would do together now that we were in a relationship.

"I'm gonna fuck you like this every night for the rest of my life, just like this. I'll make you cum on my tongue or maybe my fingers. And then you're going to cum on my cock. Every. Fucking. Night."

"You're going to sleep in my bed. And take my cock into your throat. You're all fucking mine, Fox."

"I've waited for you for my entire fucking life, and now I get to make up for the time we missed out on." He pushed into me especially hard after that comment.

I lost track of how many times I came that day, but all that mattered was that we both passed out in my bed together when the night was over. Relationship sex absolutely deserved ten stars. And Reid definitely pinched my ass for that comment.

31

Nick

A month later

Fox's arm firmly grasped my elbow as we walked into Georgia's house. Or it was Ashton and Georgia's house now, I supposed. She leaned in and gave me a quick peck on the cheek.

"I'm so excited for them." I smiled back at her and couldn't help but place my own kiss on her head.

"Me too, Ruthie is probably losing her mind right now." My brother finally proposed to his girlfriend. He tried proposing about twenty times over, but failed to make the moment right. Until this morning, hours before his own *engagement* party.

We walked through to the back yard and found Ruthie blowing bubbles with Ash and Georgia hanging up decorations around the yard. Ruth saw me first and squealed, "Uncle Nick!"

I caught her hug and spun her in a circle before placing her back down on the ground. "Fox!" Charlotte shot me a look, since I confessed to her recently that I couldn't stand when other people used my nickname for her.

She bent down and greeted Ruth before we went over to congratulate Georgia and my brother. Both of them had huge smiles and Georgia proudly waved around her ring to show Charlotte. I let the two speak before pulling Ash off to the side.

"You finally did it?" His smile took up his entire face.

He nodded and handed me a streamer to tape to a fence post. "I did. And it was fucking perfect, totally worth the wait."

"How did you do it?" I found some tape and started draping up streamers to match the work that they had already done.

"We went to the beach this morning, and Ruth held the box for me. She was totally fucking surprised." He bit off a piece of tape with his teeth. "It was great, man."

"I'm happy for you brother." We shared a quick hug before getting back to work.

The party lasted for most of the day as our closest friends came over to celebrate Ashton and Georgia. I met Georgia's sister for the first time and was hit with the fact that we were building a family. Just years ago it was only Ash and I against the world. And now we had all of these people who were more than just family.

Looking down at Fox, I imagined the day I would finally propose to her. For now, I promised to go to therapy and work on my own stuff since she had made so much progress. We were living together though, I made it clear that there wouldn't be a single night I wanted to spend apart from her. So we moved all of her stuff into my apartment.

We even signed the adoption papers for Link together, and he traveled with Fox to and from my apartment to the bookstore every morning to spend time with her at work. I was pretty fucking happy. As the day came to a close we returned home and got into bed together, just like we would every night for the rest of my damn life.

Epilogue

Charlotte

Six months later

Reid had been away for far too long, and I was starting to get antsy. The major food convention that he got invited to last month was on the west coast. He claimed that it wasn't that exciting, but I knew he was secretly dying to go, so I encouraged him to. Since it was so far, he flew out over a week ago and was due back any minute now.

My car sat in line at the airport while I waited impatiently for him to walk outside of the glass doors. Dylan was on the phone with me since we spoke on the phone every second we got, now that she was always busy with her new job. Apparently she was so fantastic at being a regional manager they promoted her to managing an entire division. I wasn't sure what the difference was, but she said it excitedly so I was happy.

"So, when are you moving to Rosewood?" Dyl laughed at the question I had asked a hundred times over in the past few months.

"Are you willing to hire me at your cafe finally?"

"Hell no, Spencer needs to keep her job. And she's a lot more reliable than you are." Dylan scoffed at the insult.

After the first month of opening Brewing Pages, I decided I needed to hire part time workers. I was working myself to the bone everyday and felt like there was no end in sight. Reid kept nagging at me, and when I finally reached out to Reese she connected me with one of my new favorite people, Spencer.

She was a high school student, and also just had a baby. The kid was absolutely adorable and she brought him to work to nap in one of those cute bouncing contraptions that babies like. Having help also meant that I got to take Saturdays off, so I'd been going to volleyball practice every weekend.

"Well, until I find a job I can't just up and move, Char. I'm responsible now. I'm a productive member of society."

"Are you sure you didn't join a cult or something?"

She laughed. A familiar figure out of the corner of my eye caught my attention. Those huge glass doors opened to reveal the man I had been waiting for far too long.

"It's not a cult, we just get together in huge gatherings and report to one, all-knowing leader." I snorted at her dumb joke.

"I have to go, Reid is here."

Dylan chuckled through the phone. "Alright, tell Benjamin I said hello!" Ever since Reid and I were official, Dyl had started this new fun nickname. Since my ex was a nickel, that made Reid the one hundred dollar bill. It was even funnier because he did not understand the joke whatsoever.

Telling her bye, I quickly got out of the car to jump into Reid's arms. We pulled back and I got to see his handsome face and that blinding smile. I missed him so damn much. I wrapped my arms around his waist tighter and squeezed as hard as I could.

"I missed you." He chuckled with his face pressed into my hair.

"I missed you too, honey," he whispered and kissed my head. Cars had been lining up for a long time, so I opened my trunk for him to throw his luggage into. Heading to my side of the car, he stopped me and held open the drivers side door for me.

Slightly blushing at the sweet action, I sunk into the seat and waited for him to join me. He got in the car and we were on our way home. A minute after we started driving, I wanted to reach over and bury my nose in his shoulder. He smelled so damn good, I missed having him around more than I'd care to ever admit. I slept in his clothes while he called me to have our pillow talk every night.

"Is that my t-shirt?" I looked down to see that it actually was. Unintentionally, I had been stealing a lot of his clothes lately.

My face turning pink at the accusation, I muttered, "Maybe."

He chuckled and pinched my cheek. "Do you think you can help me dye my hair when we get home?" His fingers combed through it. "My roots are coming in and it's fading."

At a stoplight, I smiled over at him and nodded. "Remember to tip this time, okay?"

He leaned over the center console and kissed my cheek. "Of course, Fox. You'll be well compensated for your services. Is Spencer working tomorrow?" I hummed in response. "We have plans, so we'll have to miss gym practice."

I quickly glanced his way. "What plans?"

His huge smile returned as he leaned back in his seat. "You forgot."

My heart raced as I tried to figure out what the hell he was talking about. We definitely hadn't been dating for a year yet, so I wasn't missing any anniversaries. His birthday was still a few months away. What could it possibly be?

He laughed at my concentration. "You'll find out tomorrow. Lucky for you, I happen to remember everything."

My eyes rolled and I began interrogating him on how his trip was for the rest of the ride home. The sun was setting just as we reached Rosewood. Walking into the diner, Reid gave Jace a quick hug and asked how things were while he was gone. I started playing with one of the long sleeves on Reid's t-shirt while they spent way too long catching up.

Reid threw me a knowing glance and started making food while he finished up his conversation with Jace. He handed me a plate with chicken tenders and fries while we headed upstairs to his loft. Link was waiting next to the door when we opened it and nearly knocked Reid over with his greeting.

He sank to the floor and hugged Link until he got one huge lick to the ear. "Okay, buddy. I've gotta hang out with your mom now or she's going to get jealous."

I sat at the couch and started tearing through french fries. "I am not *jealous*."

Reid snickered and sat down next to me. He laughed right in my ear and wrapped his arm around my waist. I kept my back straight and continued to focus on chowing down on food. "Jealous *and* hungry. Bad combo, honey," he teased.

"Are you not hungry?" I asked.

"Not really." He stole a couple of fries off of my plate. "I'm dying to take a shower, though. Want to join?" He smirked and nudged his nose against mine.

I swallowed the bite I was working on and gave him my full attention by accepting his kiss. "A shower sounds nice."

His grin turned wicked as he picked me up bridal style and

carried me into the bathroom. We got naked and hopped under the stream of warm water. He made sure to wash my hair because he knew how much I loved it when he did. I returned the favor by welcoming him home with my mouth.

After our shower was finished, we wound up sitting in our dry bathtub with him sitting in front of me, completely shirtless. I now wore a different short sleeved black tee of his while I carefully brushed on dark hair dye to his soft hair. The plastic gloves made it hard, but I was very precise with not getting the dye on his scalp. The first time I did this, I accidentally stained a spot on his forehead and he complained about it for weeks.

"So, how is book club going?" he asked.

Dipping the brush to get another glob of dye, I hummed. "It's good, the kids are finally getting comfortable with each other. Last week I barely spoke at all, they led the discussion on their own."

A couple months back, I decided to host a book club at the store for 'at risk' kids at Rosewood's high school. Reese helped me get in contact with the principal, and they thought it was a perfect extra credit activity for kids who were failing subjects and in danger of not graduating. They were all great kids, each one was dealing with their own issues and I did my best to give them books that they could relate to.

Running the book club gave me a lot of joy, and the kids really seemed to love Link. Teenagers used to scare me, but I knew what these kids were going through and wanted to do my best to help them. Through the club, I got to know a bit about all of them, and most of them were doing the best with what they had.

Reid turned around and I could see how exhausted he was on

his face. "Hold still, I almost got some on your ear," I grumbled.

"Just wanted to give you your tip early." He leaned in and gave me a quick peck on the lips. My smile was involuntary and I scoffed.

I waited until he returned to his position to keep brushing on the dye. "You are such a sap."

"Any luck with convincing Dyl?"

I sighed. "No, she's still all obsessed with this dumb job. The one time I need her to quit is the one time she doesn't want to do it."

He laughed at my frustration. "She'll come around eventually. I know you miss her."

Slipping off my gloves, I grabbed his head gently to tilt it all around to make sure I didn't miss any spots. "Okay, sir. You're good to go. Have a nice day."

The sound of his laugh made me smile. He faced me and pulled me into his lap for a real kiss this time. I returned it happily. We pulled back and I cupped his jaw. "You're sleepy."

He mumbled his agreement and nodded while leaning into my hand with his eyes closed. "Jet lag, and it's like 9 PM."

"Come on, old man. We can sit on the couch until we need to rinse it out." I helped him up and we resumed our favorite positions on the couch. He rested his back against the right corner of it, and opened his legs so I could scoot in and sit between them with my back to his chest.

While we waited twenty minutes for the dye to process, his thumb traced invisible shapes on one of my thighs and he held me tight to his chest with his other arm. He told me about the bachelor party he was planning for Ashton since he was his best man. They were going on a trip to Vegas while the women, including me, were going to New York to celebrate

Georgia's bachelorette party.

My alarm went off, so I helped him up and walked him to the bathtub to rinse out his hair with warm water before drying it with a towel. He almost fell asleep while I worked. I went as quickly as I could, and when I finished I helped him to bed. He sank into our king bed, falling asleep almost instantly. I say almost, because he waited for me to slide in on my side before dragging me closer to him with one of his arms.

Link hopped up on the bed too and laid between my legs with his head resting on whichever part of Reid he could reach, like usual. I stayed awake for quite some time, feeling grateful for this nice little life of mine.

* * *

I woke up to a gentle thumb stroking my cheek. My eyes opened slowly and I was greeted with one of my favorite sights, Nicholas Reid with messy hair. It was especially messy today because he fell asleep while it was still wet. His thumb traced my smile while I woke up.

"Good morning." His voice was deep and gravelly. I instantly wanted to kick Link off the bed and have my way with my boyfriend. Leaning in to do just that, he gave me a quick peck on the cheek before sitting up. I pouted and my eyebrows furrowed at the offensive action.

He chuckled, knowing exactly why I was annoyed. "Come on, we have to get up. Your breakfast is getting cold."

The place between my eyebrows managed to scrunch up even more while I tried to figure out what the hell he was being such an early riser for. At my hesitation, he leaned over to slip his hands around my waist and pulled me into a sitting position.

"Why did you make my breakfast so early? That's your fault," I complained.

With a peck on my cheek, he got up and went to the bathroom to start getting ready. I reached over to give Link some morning pets while my insane boyfriend eagerly prepared himself for whatever it was we were doing today.

He walked out of the bathroom and picked me up. "What are you doing?" My legs wrapped around his waist to steady myself. His smile made my nerves go away as he set me down on the bathroom counter.

"We've gotta get ready. Now sit still." This was one of his favorite activities. We didn't get to do it often, since we both ran businesses that opened up way too early in the morning, but every chance he got, he made sure to do my morning routine for me.

I sat perfectly still as he went through every step in my skincare routine and brushed my hair. He gave me a kiss, which was his signal that he was finished. Feeling a little less grumpy, I went to get dressed.

"Athletic clothes, baby. No dresses," he advised.

Turning around, I fixed him with a glare. "If you would tell me what we're doing, that would be very helpful, you know?"

A smile played on his lips. "You'll see."

When we were both finished getting ready, he led us to the car. He even brought Link along which made me more curious as to what the hell he was up to. Halfway through the drive I figured out we were on our way to the beach. But why?

Getting out of the car, he grabbed a volleyball out of his trunk. "Are they doing practice at the beach today?"

Volleyball practice was every Saturday, and it wasn't totally abnormal for everyone to decide to do a beach practice every once in a while. "Nope, it's just us today."

I followed him to the net and he started untying his shoes. "You might want to start stretching, Fox. I don't want any excuses this time."

Finally, the lightbulb turned on in my brain. We were having our rematch, it had been about six months since we had our one on one on this beach and I lost. Since then, I practiced a lot with the guys. It was a little annoying to only play with men, so I roped Reese into joining us every now and then.

"Alright, Reid. You're on." We both stretched and warmed up by jogging on the beach next to the water. Link was more than happy to join us as he ran into the water and made sure to shake it all off when he was standing right next to us.

When we deemed ourselves ready, we laid out a towel for Link to lay on and started up our match. The sunrise was beautiful, and we had the entire beach to ourselves. I took the first serve and landed it right in his side of the court.

We went back and forth, and I quickly realized that he was totally throwing this match. He was a God awful actor, especially because I watched him play all the damn time. His movements were slow and he wasn't trying nearly as hard as he usually did.

At match point, I had seven points on him. I had practiced a lot in the last few months, but he was totally milking this. "Why aren't you trying?" I huffed.

He smiled. "I am, you're just that good, Fox."

I spiked the ball in his court on our next rally and he laughed before running under the net and hugging me. "Next time, six months from now, I'll rewin the title of champion."

Shoving him lightly, I laughed. "In your dreams, Reid."

We shared our usual dumb lovesick smiles while he held me tightly in his arms. "I love you."

"I love you too," I whispered.

He pulled back suddenly and reached for my hand to tug me along. We collected Link and our things and returned to the car. "There's more?"

"Of course there's more, we have to go get your prize." His smile was blinding.

"Prize?" He hummed in agreement and said nothing more as we drove to our new destination.

We arrived at Georgia and Ashton's house and I looked over at Reid suspiciously. "What are you up to?"

He said nothing as he let Link out of the car and we walked hand in hand up to their door. Georgia opened it and a puppy bolted out of entryway, between her legs. "Shit, wait!" she called.

Reid reached down with his quick reflexes and scooped up the tiny ball of fur. "Surprise," he said casually as he handed the puppy to me.

"What?" I looked at the adorable thing in front of me and immediately fell in love. "I had no idea you guys got a dog, he is so cute."

I looked to Georgia and her wide eyes went back to Reid as Ashton popped up behind her. "Honey, the dog is yours. And it's a she," Reid corrected.

My head snapped to the side, trying to figure out if he was being serious. "We've talked about getting a puppy, and I figured now would be as good a time as any."

I looked back to the tiny thing that was squirming around in my arms. "She's ours?"

He chuckled and nodded. Ashton leaned in and gave the

puppy a quick scratch behind the ears. "She's a rascal, I hope you're well rested."

Totally in a haze, I let Reid say goodbye for us and we walked back to the car. Link leaned in to sniff the new puppy and my heart melted at the sight of them together. "Are you happy?"

"Of course I am, it's a fucking puppy." I snuggled into her fur and looked at Reid with puppy dog eyes. "I love you. Even if you totally let me win this morning."

"Let's take her home, I waited to buy her a ton of toys because I knew you would want to buy a mountain just like Link has." My smile widened at his thoughtfulness. This man knew me so well, and I wouldn't want to grow my little family with anyone else.

"I love you, Nicholas Reid." I couldn't say those words enough these days.

"I love you, Charlotte Fox."

ACKNOWLEDGEMENT

A special thank you to my beta readers, without you this book would not be the novel it has become. Thank you Gracia, Molly, Kelly, Davis, Whitney, Lindsay, Kasey, Lauren, Claire, Giulia, and Emily.

Made in the USA
Monee, IL
22 August 2023

41479491R00152